A police car appeared down the road to her right, lights swirling but siren off. She held tightly to her bag of doughnut holes. She suddenly understood those real-life criminals in cop videos: losers who ran when they were surrounded, ran when they were wounded, ran when they were in a dead-end alley.

Rose Lymond wanted to run.

Instead she lifted her arm straight into the air and waved it once, like a flag on a pole, to catch their attention. I have the right to remain silent, Rose said to herself. I was silent four years ago. I've been silent this week. I can be silent now.

Other Caroline B. Cooney paperbacks you will enjoy:

FATALITY

CAROLINE B. COONEY

SCHOLASTIC INC.

New York   Toronto   London   Auckland   Sydney
Mexico City   New Delhi   Hong Kong   Buenos Aires

No part of this publication may be reproduced in whole or in part,
or stored in a retrieval system, or transmitted in any form
or by any means, electronic, mechanical, photocopying, recording,
or otherwise, without written permission of the publisher.
For information regarding permission, write to Scholastic Inc.,
Attention: Permissions Department, 555 Broadway,
New York, NY 10012.

ISBN 0-439-13524-9

12 11   6/0

Printed in the U.S.A.   01

First Scholastic printing, October 2001

FATALITY

CHAPTER ONE

The police car was not locked.

When the police had thrown her diary into their squad car, they didn't even bother to slam the door. In the casual way of police, they left the car door open so they could still hear their radio squawking.

Rose stood in the front hall of her house and stared out the windows at the police car. It was white with a blue logo and the officers had left the lights swirling. By day, the lights were not as powerful as they would have been at night. They were not threatening. It was more of a circus, telling neighbors that the show was being held here, at her house.

Lying on the front passenger seat, as if it didn't matter, was Rose's diary.

It mattered.

Suppose she walked out of the house, crossed the grass, reached into the police car, and took it back.

Robbing the police. It was dangerous, but not as dangerous as letting them read the diary.

They don't have my permission to touch that diary, she thought. My mother just went and got it. I didn't say anybody could have it. It's my property. I'm not an adult, of course. I won't be sixteen for a few months. So perhaps technically it is my mother's property and she does have the right to give it to the police and they do have the right to drive off with it.

Rose hated herself for keeping a diary. How could she have written it all down?

Stupid, stupid.

And now it would become public property. Evidence in a trial. It would be read out loud. The world would hear every word Rose Lymond had set down on paper.

She imagined talk shows: local — regional — national. Radio and television and newspapers. The teasers: *Kid's diary tells all.* Nobody would pass that up.

Rose's heart hurt. I've ruined our lives, she thought.

In the formal living room, rarely used, her parents were pacing back and forth. Rose had been told to wait in the study. She had not argued. She had not shouted, "I'm not a child. I prefer to stay!" Instead, she walked quietly into the front hall and out of sight. They expected her to continue on through the house and sit in the study, surrounded by books and silent papers.

But papers were not silent. She herself had produced the noisiest paper of all. Paper that would shout the truth. Truth she could never permit anybody to know.

The police were bored and ready to leave. She had little time in which to make her decision.

If she were to slip out the front door, the adults would neither see nor hear her. She could walk across the grass toward the driveway and they would not see or hear that, either. The police car itself, however, was visible from the long, tall row of living room windows.

But now the discussion among the grown-ups was becoming heated. Perhaps nobody was gazing out a window. She could race across the grass, lean into the police car, snatch the diary, and run. Or walk slowly, bending calmly over to retrieve what was, after all, her own property.

Either way, Rose could reach the diary before anybody could leave the house and stop her.

Then what?

She could run, Rose supposed. Dart out into the road and race madly around the neighborhood.

Then what?

Getting the diary back was not enough. Rose had to destroy the pages. That might take time.

Other than sprinting after her, she did not think the police would do much. They were bigger and stronger, though, and could simply wrench the diary out of her hands. She wouldn't have time to bury it. There was no handy river in which to chuck it. She had no fire in which to burn it. In any event, lab techniques were astounding. Partially damaged words might be retrieved. She had to destroy those pages utterly and completely, and she did not know how.

Rose assessed her situation.

She had her house key in the pocket of her jeans. She had a dollar and some change in the other pocket. She had a stick of gum. And her library card, because she had been thinking, just before the police arrived, just before the end of the world hit her in the face, that she was in the mood for a really long read, six or seven hundred pages of suspense and terror. Rose only liked books where the good guys won.

It was difficult for Rose to tell whether she herself was a good guy. Nor was it clear how she could win.

Rose opened the front door gently and stepped outside. She closed the door softly behind her. She thought the people inside had been talking too loudly to have heard.

Rose Lymond stood on the top step of the four wide slate slabs that led down to the grass and the pretty slate-and-brick walk. The front entry to the house was beautifully designed but rarely used. People came in the side, where a sweet, narrow porch with a low white railing and boxes of yellow pansies beckoned.

Rose walked over the grass. It was soft and bouncy. Spring grass, full-of-life grass. It was early May, only six more weeks left of sophomore year. Almost four years ago, the summer before seventh grade began, Rose had started that diary.

A twelfth-birthday present from her great-grandparents, the diary was distinctive, crimson red leather with page edges dipped in gold. It looked like something handmade in London a century ago. Grandfather and Nannie had also given her a fountain pen and a glass bottle of black ink.

Rose was left-handed and could not write cleanly except with a pencil, so she never filled the fountain pen but left it, pristine in its package, on her desk. She wrote in the diary, however, from her birthday, June 28, until November 11, when it was necessary to stop.

She had never written another word in that journal or any other. She no longer knew why she had kept this one. It was a terrible mistake to keep something that told the truth.

The leather binding of the journal she could not destroy. But the pages themselves — yes. What she needed was time to shred those pages into tiny pieces and then burn or flush or throw them away in such a manner that nobody could find the shreds and piece them together.

All these things Rose thought in the course of a dozen grass-springy steps.

And then she saw that not only was the police car unlocked and the door wide open . . . the keys were hanging from the ignition.

They could not follow her if she had their car.

She didn't have much driving experience. On the other hand, people got out of your way when you were driving a police car.

Rose could drive toward the city, stop in some parking lot along the highway, shred her pages, go into some fast-food restaurant, enter the ladies' room, flush her shreds away, and it would be over.

Well, over except for the part about stealing a police car.

Rose looked back at the house. The adults were far too busy to glance out a window. They were not even near the windows.

Rose Lymond got into the police car, slammed the door, and drove away.

CHAPTER TWO

The police car was filled with gadgets and dials, speakers and buttons. It smelled of sweat and dog. Although a computer screen filled the space between the two front seats, a clipboard and notebook lay on the passenger seat, open and vulnerable like her diary.

The policeman who drove this car was much taller than Rose. She could barely touch the accelerator with the tip of her right shoe. She had little control, and if she had to brake quickly, she'd have to lift herself off the seat to jam her foot down.

She drove for a couple of miles at twenty miles an hour. Her hands were sweating so badly that the steering wheel was wet. It was disgusting. It had never happened to her before.

The police radio began to chat and she could tell that it was addressing her by name, but she didn't answer and couldn't actually hear. Either there was a lot of static in the radio or a lot of static in her brain.

The Frontage Road between the town and the highway was lined with fast-food places. She crept into a parking lot and just stopped, not bothering with a parking space. She was so eager to get out of the vehicle that she left the diary inside and had to lean back in and reach across the sweat-damp vinyl to pick it up.

She left the engine idling and the driver door open, just the way the police had.

She chose Burger King, went in the side entrance, and walked into the ladies' room. The regular stall was occupied so she went into the handicapped space, where there was more room to think anyway, and ripped out the last dozen pages of the diary, her eyes racing over the words, making sure she had the crucial details. If he knew, it would kill him. She tore half the pages savagely into strips and then into confetti and flushed them away.

"Are you out of paper?" said a kindly voice in the next stall. "Here, I'll hand some under the divider."

Rose fled.

Outdoors, her police car continued to idle and people continued to drive in and out of the parking lots. She walked between little button-shaped bushes, sinking in brown mounds of mulch that surrounded them, and over to the Mobil station. Here she got the key to the ladies' room, flushed some more paper down there, and leaving the key in the door without returning it, walked straight to Wendy's.

She shredded the last few pages into their toilet.

Next she went into the laundromat.

Rose had not often been in a laundromat. Her mother actually loved laundry and even loved ironing, claiming that ironing a dinner napkin was very satisfying, the only activity in life where you could make something perfect in twenty seconds.

Once during a hurricane, when they lost power and water for four days, Rose and Mom had come here to do the washing. The kind of person who frequented laundromats in this town was down-and-out, poor and struggling.

Rose looked at the tired, sagging women folding mountains of children's clothing and heaps of ragged towels. They could have been the same women she had met during the hurricane. She walked out the back door, because laundromats always had back entrances. Parked in two messy rows were old cars: a sad and dented Taurus station wagon, a beat-up Chevy van, an ancient rusted-out AMC hatchback, and a once-grand Town Car.

The Lincoln was filled with overflowing cardboard boxes, a tricycle without wheels, large tied plastic bags, stacks of yellowing magazines, and stuffed animals losing their stuffing. Either the owner was collecting tag sale rejects or was so fond of her junk that she stored it in the car.

The car wasn't locked. Rose opened its back door, untied a garbage bag, stuck the diary in, tied the bag back up, shut the car door, and walked around two other buildings to go into Dunkin' Donuts.

She was fading. A little sugar would help. Even at Dunkin' Donuts, a dollar and some change did not buy much. Rose chose a mixture of jelly-filled, cinnamon, and powdered-sugar doughnut holes. She pulled two large white napkins out of the dispenser, walked outside with her white paper bag, and looked around.

She should put distance between herself and the police car, the flushed toilets, and the Lincoln Town Car.

The fast-food places on Frontage Road backed up to warehouses, and beyond those, the city began. She could walk through the warehouse delivery yards, circle the big steel buildings, cross the next street, and be only a block from the library and the art gallery and the coffee shop where people sat for hours.

But what would be the point? The only place to go now was home.

Or jail.

Her legs were trembling. It was difficult to stand. Rose sat down on one of the small round white tables at the edge of the parking lot, facing the road and resting her feet on the weather-stained bench. The fringe of a faded sun umbrella shaded her eyes.

She could not eat the doughnuts after all. She pleated the bag between her fingers, spindling long wrinkly lines through the paper, until she had created a mountain range of crinkles on the doughnut bag.

She hoped it would be the police who picked her up and not her parents. She did not care about the police. She cared about her father and mother. The important thing was that they should never understand.

Indeed, they never were going to understand the theft of a car.

She knew kids whose parents didn't let them take

blame for anything, whose parents yelled and fought and hired lawyers when their kids did something wrong, insisting it wasn't really wrong, or there were extenuating circumstances, or the witnesses had lied.

Rose's parents were not of this variety.

They had not bailed her older brother, now in college, out of jail the night he and a carload of friends were stopped, driving drunk. Everybody else's parents had. But the Lymonds, furious and ashamed, said a night in jail was just what Tabor deserved.

Rose did not want a night in jail.

She rather thought that stealing a police car meant several nights in jail. Possibly weeks or months.

I can handle it, she told herself. Stealing a police car means temporary punishment. Telling the truth is a life sentence.

A police car appeared down the road to her right, lights swirling but siren off. She held tightly to her bag of doughnut holes. She suddenly understood those real-life criminals in cop videos: losers who ran when they were surrounded, ran when they were wounded, ran when they were in a dead-end alley.

Rose Lymond wanted to run.

Instead she lifted her arm straight into the air and waved it once, like a flag on a pole, to catch their attention. I have the right to remain silent, Rose said to herself. I was silent four years ago. I've been silent this week. I can be silent now.

Bits of television played through her head, an electric storm of TV cop shows, men and women in blue, attack dogs and guns, officers' adrenaline pumped so high that they gasped and heaved while the weapon in their hands somehow stayed steady. In voices too loud, charged with fear and fury, invariably they shouted, "*You have the right to remain silent. Anything you say can and will be used against you.*"

My only ally is a Supreme Court decision, thought Rose.

The police saw her, put on a turn signal, and came slowly into the Dunkin' Donuts lot, the car pulling almost close enough to amputate her legs at the knees before it stopped. The cop had his phone up to his mouth.

No. It was a woman — young, tall, and tanned. Her name tag said Megan Moran. She looked at Rose in exasperation. "Your plan?" said Megan Moran acidly as she got out of her car and walked over. "Your hopes? Your expectations? Stealing a police car?"

A second police car appeared from the other direction, entering Burger King to pull up next to the idling vehicle Rose had abandoned.

"I just needed it for a minute," Rose said. "I would have taken a different car if there'd been one with the keys in it." This was not a good beginning for somebody who intended to remain silent.

The policewoman looked Rose over, opened the wrinkled white bag, found only holes, handed it back, and sat on the tabletop next to her. "You are one dumb kid," she said.

They sat together while the afternoon sun warmed

Rose's face, and she tried to think silent, shrugging thoughts, but there was nothing to shrug about.

Two more police cars arrived. The policemen who had been in her living room were not among the ones who surrounded her now. They had lost their transportation. It was probably not a good thing to humiliate a policeman.

"Rose Lymond?" said one of them.

He was her parents' age. Rose did not know why this surprised her. She nodded. His tag said Craig Gretzak. It was a sharp, edgy name, but the man seemed mild. "Must be quite an important diary," he said next, not looking at her face but at her hand. Rose looked down, too, and saw with surprise that her hand was shaking so badly the bag was noisy, paper rustling and doughnut holes thudding softly against one another.

With difficulty she set the bag on the little white table and folded her arms across her chest.

"Where is the diary?" asked Megan Moran.

Rose said nothing. She reminded herself of her strategy, the one word a long thin repeating line *silencesilencesilencesilencesilence* until it became a hiss, a snake in her heart.

It occurred to her that the police had no idea what to do next.

They hadn't known what to do back at her house, either. When Rose said, "I don't remember, I wasn't looking, I can't think of anything," the police were stymied. Rose had drifted away, heading for the kitchen, planning on a glass of lemonade. The month of May had started out surprisingly hot and they were drinking summer drinks already. Her mother was a pink lemonade person and her father a yellow. Rose liked to cut hers half and half with seltzer to make lemonade soda pop.

From the kitchen, she had heard her mother say, "You know what? Rose kept a diary that year. I'll just run and get it. Perhaps there's something in the diary that would jog Rose's memory." Her mother's light feet raced up the stairs. Mom was never leisurely; she usually had a hundred things to do. She did them well and quickly.

Rose had pressed the lemonade glass against the automatic ice dispenser and watched as crushed ice fell into the pale yellow drink. She was astonished at the trespass. How could her mother even think of handing over somebody else's diary, let alone without asking? She took a sip of sparkly lemonade before going out to stop her mother and then she choked, the lemonade suddenly thick, gagging slime.

She remembered what was in the diary.

Rose stumbled out of the kitchen, trying to call her mother, trying not to raise her voice, trying to save them quietly, there in the hall by the stairs, but Mom had already trotted back down and Rose in her panic spilled lemonade on the thick celery-green carpet. She looked down at it, already soaking in, and thought of paper towels, while her mother said, "Here it is," and the policeman said, "Thanks."

Rose went into the formal living room, lemonade

sticky on her hand, and managed to provide two good arguments, although not the real one. "The diary is mine and it's private. I'd like it back, please."

She was shaking with horror. Her parents did not see this. They thought she was being rude and difficult. The cop's eyes, however, grew bright and interested and he looked thoughtfully down at the diary Rose Lymond did not want him reading.

"Rose," said her father, "you were a little girl when you scribbled in it, but this is not a little girl situation. They are reopening a murder case. You might have seen something you've forgotten. There might be a reference to it in your journal and they need that."

The policeman went out to his car, tossing Rose's diary in to make it irrevocably his.

"You can't let them have it," Rose said, frantic and trapped.

"Rose," said her mother, "there's probably some silly embarrassing seventh-grade gossip in those entries, but the point —"

"The point is it's my diary!"

Her parents were not used to Rose arguing with them. They were affronted. "Rose, wait in the study," said her mother stiffly, "while we settle this. I am not impressed with your childish behavior."

Her mother. Accusing Rose of childish behavior.

As Rose left the living room, the policeman returned, and it was then Rose realized that the diary was not irrevocably in the possession of the police. She could repossess it.

And she had.

Now Rose became aware that her head was between her knees. She was sitting on a little white table looking down at the long, soiled laces of her oldest sneakers. The policewoman was saying, "Take a deep breath, Rose. Don't faint on us. We're going to give you a ride home. We'll talk when we get there."

She saw the shining shoes of police feet, bits of trash, sparkles of glass from a broken taillight. She took the deep breath. They were right. She must not faint. She had to be in control of what happened next.

Craig Gretzak escorted her, as if she were his date, or a convict, to his car.

Rose Lymond, age fifteen, honor student, field hockey star, soprano, camp counselor, and baby-sitter was placed in the back of a police car to look out windows that did not roll down, above doors that did not have handles.

CHAPTER THREE

The officer had just put his car into gear when a woman lurched out of the laundromat. "She stuck this in my car!" said the woman, waving Rose's diary. The woman was scandalized, as if Rose had spray-painted obscenities on her old Lincoln. "She opened my door!" shouted the woman. "I knew she was up to no good."

Megan Moran took the diary and thanked the angry woman for her vigilance and concern. It took a few minutes to coax her to go back in and do another load of laundry. Then Megan Moran leaned her elbows on the passenger side front window of Craig Gretzak's car, open for the fresh flowery breeze of May. She leafed through the diary, every now and then glancing at Rose through the dividing grille. "So this isn't the kind of diary with the little slots for each day, Rose. Or even one page for each day. This is a journal where you decide if the day is worth two sentences or two pages and you date the entries yourself." The policewoman flipped through it slowly, reading phrases here and there. "Something written here is worth a criminal charge?"

Go ahead, Megan Moran, thought Rose. Scour the pages that are left. None of what is left matters.

Although of course it all mattered.

How shocking seventh grade had been, after the sweet friendships of sixth. Seventh graders traveled in packs: cruel, exclusionary, and circling, like jackals. They closed for the kill on losers caught alone. She remembered writing about the very fat kid nobody would sit near, the rest of the class preferring to laugh out loud and point. In sixth grade Rose would have made the effort to be his friend. In seventh, she could not bring herself to overrule the majority. She had written about the cafeteria and the risk of sitting alone; how essential to line up lunch company before approaching the meal. She had written more about the parties to which she had not been invited than the parties she had attended.

She had written about a boy on whom she had a crush so deep it embarrassed her. Even then, she used a single initial instead of his name. About spending the night at Chrissie's house, and being upset by Jill, who was also there, and jealous of Halsey, who at all times was more trendy, more knowledgeable, and more interesting than the rest of them.

It's okay, she said to herself. All they have now is a little girl's diary and all they can read are a little girl's thoughts.

"'Dear Diary,'" read Megan Moran in a pleasant voice, "'today, June 28, is my twelfth birthday, and you are my present from Grandfather and Nannie Lymond.' Are those your father's parents, Rose?"

Actually they were her father's *grand*parents. Grandfather had since died, at the age of eighty-four, but Nan-

18

nie, now eighty-six, was still bounding around. She had just given up tennis last year.

Rose wondered what Nannie was going to have to say about the car theft. Perhaps nobody would tell her. And what about her grandparents, whom she still called Popsy and Mopsy? Dad would have to tell them because on Sunday, Popsy and Mopsy would bring Nannie along for dinner after church. Nannie had been a member of the same Bible class for sixty-one years. What would Nannie think of Rose? What would everybody say, gathered around the table with their suddenly juvenile delinquent granddaughter? Or would they say nothing?

Rose felt she could say nothing just fine.

"You made entries all the way up to November, Rose. And here I am, closing in on November 8, the murder date, and you've ripped out ten or twelve pages." Megan Moran squinted, counting the shreds that were left in the binding. "You flush them down the toilet?"

Rose said nothing.

"And then no more entries. After the ripped-out pages, the rest of the diary is blank. So you didn't write in the diary again after you witnessed the murder, huh, Rose?"

Rose closed her eyes for a while, the way she did at the movies during rough parts. Nannie adored action movies and when Rose spent the night, Nannie always chose a movie with high bloodshed levels so she and Rose could scream together.

I handled this so stupidly, she thought. I should have acted like the twelve-year-old who wrote "Dear Diary." Bitten my lip and giggled and blushed. I should have said, "I wasn't nice to other seventh graders and I don't want you to see my mean little thoughts." I should have said, "Really and truly, I'm just embarrassed about this silly old diary." They would have believed me. I would have gotten away with it. But no, I had to make a scene.

"So, Rose," said Craig Gretzak, "you never wrote in the diary again after the murder? You know what, Rose? I think we'll go down to the station after all."

He drove at a leisurely pace that required every other driver on Frontage Road to brake. Rose slumped in the back. It was the posture of defeat. No, she thought. I'm going to win. I have to win. I have secrets to keep.

She sat bolt upright, took in the scenery, and planned her silence.

At the police department, they did not take Rose into any jail-style rooms. The room they picked was quite pleasant, sun streaming through windows and bars to make a nice diamond pattern on the floor.

They waited for her parents and a lawyer to arrive. The lawyer would probably be Kate Bering, who lived down the road, and who had been setting out pink-and-white begonias in her garden when Rose had come home from school. While her kids were little, Kate had all but abandoned her practice and did only quick, basic stuff a few hours a week. She'd be delighted to be brought into something unusual, and what's more, she'd hardly even yell at Rose. Kate liked gumption in a woman.

The officers chatted. "Rose, honey, if the diary is so bad," said one man, "why did you still have it?"

This was an excellent question, and one to which she had no answer, so Rose said, "Please don't call me 'honey.'"

"I apologize, Rose. I won't say it again."

"Rose, we have to charge you with stealing a vehicle," said Megan Moran, "and driving without a license. But you're a juvenile, the circumstances are unusual, and you probably won't get a severe punishment. If you'll help us with this, Rose, we'll help you with the judge when you talk to him."

Rose planned to be silent with the judge as well.

Into the room came the two policemen from whose squad car she had taken the diary and in whose squad car she had left home.

Stealing, it was called. She decided not to look at them.

"Rose," said Megan Moran, "you do know that a woman died. I want you to think about her, instead of yourself. She was thirty-nine. She didn't die of old age. She didn't die of natural causes. She died in fear and pain. You are allowing the murderer to get away with it."

"I am not!" said Rose fiercely. "You don't understand! You —" She caught herself.

The police were softly waiting, like bunnies in the

garden, but they would turn into foxes if she kept talking.

I cannot justify myself! I'm giving little pieces of myself away. Silence is the only weapon I have. In other words, Rose, she said to herself, shut up.

"Rose, we understand that you want to protect people. But if those people are murderers, it's wrong of you. An innocent woman is dead. We know you can tell us what happened."

Rose held herself very still. They would get no body language from her. No verbal language, either.

"Would you like a Coke, Rose? We don't want you getting woozy again."

Fainting might be good after all. With any luck she could tip over, hit her head, and be hospitalized. That would spare her dealing with her parents and a judge. Nurses were bound to be kinder.

She wondered how she was going to deal with her mother and father. They had had their hands full on several occasions with Tabor, but Rose as a rule came through for them. In part, she was naturally easier than her brother and in part, she enjoyed being the nice one, but also she wasn't attracted to the edgy activities that drew Tabor.

She missed her brother suddenly and painfully. His departure for college had left a great hole in the family and they had not entirely gotten over it. Dutiful Rose was not a substitute for star-material Tabor.

"You've gone pretty far just to hide a few lines scribbled in a kid's diary," said Megan Moran. "I'm beginning to wonder, Rose, if you yourself had something to do with the murder."

Rose was so astonished she almost forgot her vow of silence and began to explain. *You don't understand. It didn't happen that way. I wasn't part of anything.*

But the police would say, How *did* it happen? What *was* it part of?

Her parents walked in, and it was not Kate Bering they had brought. It was Mr. Travis, the criminal lawyer they had used that time they were here with Tabor.

They think I need a major league lawyer, thought Rose, her heart sinking.

Mom had been crying. Dad was red and puffy with fury, which was good, because if he'd been weepy, she would have wept with him and been weakened.

Neither of them knew how to greet her. Do you hug and kiss a daughter you're meeting in the police station because she stole a car?

"Rose," said her father, gripping both her shoulders, "you'd better have one good reason for doing this."

Since she did of course have one good reason, his anger only strengthened her resolve. "I'm sorry, Daddy, but that was my diary, and nobody has a right to read it, and nobody had a right to take it. Including Mom. So I took it back."

"And a police car with it! Are you proud of what you've done for some lousy paragraph in some childish old journal?"

Rose thought this kind of conversation could probably go on for a while, and she was right. Rose returned to silence. Time passed unpleasantly.

"Do you think this is a film set?" shouted her mother. "Cut the drama!"

Rose remained silent.

"Rose," said Craig Gretzak finally.

Everybody must be getting pretty sick of her name. One syllable, over and over. Rose, Rose, Rose.

"Let's review that time span," said the policeman. "Anjelica Lofft invited you to spend the weekend at her father's retreat."

Rose had never imagined herself being friends with Anjelica. Even in seventh grade, Rose was academic, a trait that separated her from Anjelica's crowd. The invitation had been astonishing and wonderful. Rose was filled with excitement and pride that Anjelica had chosen her, instead of interesting and worthy girls like Chrissie or Jill or Halsey, who were quick to pooh-pooh the coming weekend. They pointed out that Anjelica used up friends quickly; that perhaps it would be more truthful to say Anjelica had no friends, merely acquaintances she adopted and discarded in the course of a week or a month. In a dark seventh-grade corner of her heart, Rose thoroughly enjoyed their jealousy.

"You were thrilled, Rose," said Megan Moran. "Anyone would be. The Loffts are a big deal. You told all your friends about it. Mr. Lofft and Anjelica planned to pick you up late Friday afternoon and drive to their lake house."

The Loffts owned the whole lake and the mountain behind it. They owned every one of the cars in their sixteen-car garage. The girls were only twelve, but Mr. Lofft had promised they could drive any of the cars as long as they stayed in the compound. Maybe go up in his private plane. Preview a movie that had not yet hit the theaters. Ride horses from his stable.

"That Friday," said the policeman, "when you left school, you walked two blocks to the Y for swim class."

It startled Rose that he knew about swim class.

Actually, she had skipped swimming that Friday because Aunt Sheila had been visiting. Rose's family lived on the East Coast, and Aunt Sheila on the West, so they did not see a lot of each other. Aunt Sheila and Mom were on the phone a lot and e-mailed almost every day, but years could go by without a real visit. Rose used to wonder how Aunt Sheila could stand to be alone for Thanksgiving and Christmas. But Aunt Sheila did not seem to notice family holidays, either as family or as holidays. Sometimes she sent Rose and Tabor fabulous presents, and sometimes she forgot entirely.

Aunt Sheila had been hurt that Rose had better things to do for the weekend than stay home and visit. If seventh grade taught Rose nothing else, it made clear the agony of being set aside for somebody better. She had decided to spend the hour of swim class with Aunt Sheila instead, to make up for deserting her.

Rose walked home, thinking what to pack her clothes in. She had an adorable little suitcase of fake leather, covered with fake travel stickers of the kind used a century ago by ladies going to Cairo or Vienna. But Anjelica had probably *really* gone to Cairo or Vienna and her suitcases were probably real leather. She might laugh at Rose.

In seventh grade, the very worst thing was to be laughed at.

That left a backpack bought new for seventh grade, stunning, vivid purple, with a dozen zippered pockets and compartments. But lockers were back in style and nobody was using backpacks anymore. Rose carried it to school only once.

Was a purple backpack a good choice? If you actually were a cool person, like Anjelica, as opposed to Rose, who hadn't figured it out yet (and as it turned out, never did), would you think the backpack was cool? Rose dawdled on the road, recognizing that she had not the slightest desire to talk to Aunt Sheila. She wanted to be alone with her packing and her excitement.

The voice of the policeman penetrated her mind once more. "Milton Lofft came for you about four-thirty, didn't he, Rose?"

Four years ago, when the police asked her about Milton Lofft, Rose hadn't even known that was his first name. She told them she didn't know anybody named Milton.

"In a Lincoln Navigator, wasn't it?" said the current policeman, just like the policeman of four years ago.

Typical luxury SUV brute. It hadn't even been a decent color. It was just brown. It lumbered over the road like a bear from the forest.

Inside, the Navigator was huge, with a custom interior. Behind the driver were two swivel seats facing a VCR that was flanked by containers of movies, books, board games with magnetic playing pieces, and hand-held computer games. Mr. Lofft listened to a book on tape while Anjelica had put a movie in the VCR. There were headphones, so they didn't have to listen to each other's choices, but they didn't bother. Mr. Lofft smoked cigars, a habit Rose knew only from cartoons. The smoke had a sweet, woodsy scent, as if they were camping and somebody would soon bring out the marshmallows. Anjelica had a special blanket, pillow, and stuffed bear. She tucked up and fell asleep without once chatting with Rose.

High above traffic in the bulky Navigator, Rose had stared out the window at the darkening shadows of early autumn. Ninety miles of driving ahead of them. The voices and plots of book and movie spun through Rose, all these dialogues later to mix crazily with the first round of police questioning. And now, sitting dizzily amid the clamor and anger of parents and police, Rose could hardly tell whether the police voice speaking so sharply was the one she remembered from four years ago or a voice in the present.

But Mr. Lofft stopped on the way to the lake to talk to somebody, didn't he, Rose? He went through a stone gate and up a private cobblestone drive. Tell us about the house on the hill, Rose.

The house, imitating its site, had been steeply slanted, surrounded by rock cuts, twisted trees, and a real waterfall from a real brook. "Does the house span the brook?" Rose had asked Mr. Lofft, astonished. It was the only thing she had said to him so far.

"Yup. Glass floor in the living room looks down on the waterfall. It's a famous house. I'll be right back. Gotta yell at Frannie." He slammed his car door and strode toward the house. The landscaping and shadows closed in on him.

Anjelica lifted her head briefly.

"Who is Frannie?" asked Rose.

"Business partner. They've been together ten years and they've never had a nice conversation. All they do is yell. We can probably hear from here. Want something to eat? There's lots of food."

The girls knelt on the floor to look in a tiny fridge where there were cold soft drinks and some grapes. A wicker basket lined with checked red cotton held fat bakery cookies and triangular pastries. A grocery bag overflowed with chip selections.

Pipe smoke had settled toward the floor and Rose coughed. "I'm not hungry," she said, returning to her seat.

Anjelica, still kneeling, tore open a bag of blue corn chips.

Rose, did Mr. Lofft go inside the house?

I don't know.

Did you go inside the house?

No.

Rose, did you hear the argument between Mr. Lofft and Ms. Bailey?

I can't remember.

Rose, it's important. Try to remember.

I think Anjelica and I were having a snack. I think she opened blue corn chips.

What time did you arrive at the lake estate?

After dark.

Did Mr. Lofft stop for any other errands or any other reason?

Traffic, I think. There was a lot of traffic.

Did you have dinner with Mr. Lofft?

I don't remember.

It was this answer that made the police so unwilling to believe Rose. The police said that a twelve-year-old could have been so busy giggling with her girlfriend that she paid no attention to the ride; okay, they could live with that. But dinner at so impressive an estate as Milton Lofft's? It must have been exciting and memorable. She could not have forgotten her welcome dinner at a mansion literally five times the size of her own home.

But in fact there had been no dinner, just a lot of food laid out on a long counter that gleamed like a waxed car. Cold salads with bright, unusual greens; a leg of lamb, sliced and steaming; beautifully garnished unknown hot dishes; a cold chicken surrounded by lemon slices; hot breads in twists and braids; cheese and fruit in artistic arrangements.

"Eat whenever you want," said Anjelica. "Like on a cruise ship."

"Don't you sit down together?" asked Rose.

19

"Only if we have guests." Anjelica apparently did not think of Rose as a guest, just a person who was there. Never glancing at the nutritional food, Anjelica helped herself to a slice of the richest, most lavishly iced and decorated chocolate cake Rose had ever seen, and wandered off with her plate.

And like a cruise ship, the place featured lots of activities. Rose discovered in the course of the weekend that she could watch a movie in the entertainment room, swim in the heated indoor pool, swim in the heated outdoor pool. Enjoy the game room, the craft room, the book room. Sit in the solarium, visit the orchid greenhouse, ride horses, play with the new litter of puppies in the kennels.

There weren't, however, lots of people. Half the time, she couldn't even find Anjelica or Mr. Lofft. Rose kept feeling that if she just went around one more corner, she would find the party, but she never did.

Now the cop's voice tightened. His brittle anger yanked Rose into the present. "Rose, a good kid with an outstanding academic record doesn't lightly steal a police car. In fact, darn few people, no matter what their grades in school, have ever committed that particular crime. And darn few people actually stay silent, Rose. People love to be at the center of things, talking away, being important. You can't come up with a single detail about two and a half days at a billionaire's lake estate? Rose, I have some photographs I want you to see. I want you to see the dead woman's body. It wasn't found for several days, you know. I want you to see it swollen and grotesque and covered with maggots and know that you are protecting the person who did this to her."

"No!" cried her father, voice strangled in his throat. He backed himself and Rose against the wall to prevent his daughter from having to look at such photographs. He was trembling. "But Rose, honey," he said, and the whole room had to stop breathing in order to hear him talk, because his voice was so papery thin, "if you saw a murder, how could you go on to play games, and drive antique cars, and laugh with another little girl? I can't believe you're so callous and yet I don't know how to believe anything else. I have to agree with the police. You must have witnessed something you are refusing to tell us. Or why destroy what you wrote about *that* weekend, and *only* that weekend?"

His faith in Rose as a good person was cracking. His faith in himself as a good parent was cracking.

Rose shivered with what she had done to them all.

And then reminded herself that *she* was not the one who had done it.

Mr. Travis — finally acting like a lawyer — said that enough was enough. They would return the following day to meet with the juvenile court judge.

"Tomorrow?" said Rose dizzily.

Surely she had heard on some TV news show that it was a real scandal the way people had to wait weeks and months for their trials to be scheduled. How could they possibly fit Rose in the very next day? Why couldn't she be part of this scheduling scandal and have to wait weeks and months?

Anyway, she had school.

The police read her mind. "This is not so much a car-stealing case as a murder case, Rose. They'll fit you in right away. You have a lot of explaining to do."

CHAPTER FOUR

But no matter how much explaining Rose Lymond had to do, she didn't do any of it.

Dinner was just awful.

She was so stunned by what she had done that she could hardly lift her fork.

Her parents were so stunned by what she had done that they could barely keep from throwing their forks. They had only one question. *What is this all about?*

She had only one answer. *Nothing.*

Rose did not sleep but trembled on the surface of sleep.

Darkness and night, which she usually loved, seemed full of the monsters of childhood.

For breakfast, she had a single piece of dark toast, lightly buttered. It was bland, but the moment she finished chewing, it churned inside her.

"Be at the front door of the school at eleven," said her mother.

Rose said nothing, and then thought, That way is trouble. So she said, "Mom, I'm truly sorry you and Dad have to deal with this. Don't be mad, please. I'll be on time. I promise." With an effort, she looked into her mother's eyes and with great effort, kissed her mother's cheek.

She fled to the bus. Middle-school kids took a bus and sometimes ninth and tenth graders, but juniors and seniors would rather quit high school than be caught on a bus. They owned a car, their friends owned a car, or their parents drove them. Rose, therefore, was the oldest on her bus. The one who should set the good example.

So much for that, thought Rose.

The bus was so crowded that kids sat on each other's laps. It made for a loud, bruising camaraderie from which nobody could be left out. It was restful to be jammed into so many conversations and bodies.

In elementary school, Rose had made friends easily. School swarmed with friends: her friends, other people's friends, future friends. There were kids she did not want to know better and kids she wished she'd never met, but mostly, Rose was surrounded by people she liked. Her whole problem was finding enough time to spend with each of them.

Then came the terrible interlude of seventh and eighth. There almost wasn't anything you could call friendship. People weren't nice enough to be friends. Every few weeks you'd identify a different girl as your best friend, but in actual fact, it was only a girl you didn't happen to be scornful of at the moment. Kids moved through school like fish, flashing through the halls, turning into piranhas to attack one kid, into minnows to follow another.

Then came freshman year in high school. Kids who

had treated Rose like a toxic waste site were nice again. Sophomore year was positively civilized. Rose knew herself to be popular, or at least cheerfully tolerated.

Which itself was a problem. Friendship was based on telling everything. She had to face her friends and tell them nothing. Shocked, they would say, You stole a police car? Laughing nervously, they would demand, You tell us every detail! They'd be fascinated. But Rose would have to be silent with them, and unlike parents and police and lawyers and probably the judge, her classmates would not let it go. Silence would be an insult that friendship could not withstand.

Eighty students clambered out of one bus and Rose Lymond prepared for the onslaught of questions.

The week after her visit to the Loffts, every acquaintance had lined up, demanding details. Everybody wanted to know if the fabulous estate was really fabulous and the great adventure really something to be jealous of. If Rose had been a clever liar, she would have come up with some great adventure. But all she could say was, Nothing happened.

By the end of that terrible week, the murder and her possible connection to it had been made known. Now the demands for information were ceaseless, her classmates hoping Rose would be a pivotal witness in a glamorous trial. How disgusted they were with her responses, how unwilling to accept her boring statement: *Nothing happened.*

Today, Rose reached her locker before it dawned on her that nobody knew about yesterday. Just because it had shattered her life didn't mean it had been on TV or radio or in the papers. Just because police lights had swirled in her front yard didn't mean that neighbors had been home, or noticed, or gossiped. Perhaps the car theft would never be made public, since she was a juvenile and had privacy rights not accorded to adults.

"Rose!" bellowed Ming. Ming was Chinese, adopted in infancy, and had the smallest bones of anybody in school, but the largest voice. "You didn't answer my e-mail yesterday!" yelled Ming. "You weren't sick, were you? You're never sick."

In her lifetime, Rose had not failed to check her messages. Yesterday *had* been traumatic.

Emma said, "You know perfectly well her family went somewhere cool and she was too busy for us. We never go anywhere. I want to be born again in your family, Rose."

"Did you finish your botany project, Rose?" asked Caitlin. "I had to ask for an extension. I'm dead, because even with an extension, I'm not going to have enough to turn in."

She, Rose, academic from her pencil tip to her laptop, had forgotten her homework. She felt unhinged, like a door that no longer closes.

The girls hurtled into school together, unaware that Rose was not participating in the talk.

Richard caught up to them. Alex. Keith. And far down the hall, Chrissie was shouldering two huge bags, one for books, one for sports equipment.

Rose would have written more about Chrissie in the

diary than anybody else because they had been best best best friends in elementary school and from habit went on seeing each other in middle. But they had grown apart. Chrissie was ferociously athletic, eager to be a basketball star and play on a winning college team, like UConn or Tennessee. If Chrissie was not practicing layups, she was on the rowing machine or lifting free weights or swimming laps. She also studied fiercely, not because she cared about her subjects but so she'd be referred to as a basketball star taking premed instead of a basketball star taking remedial math.

Ming was a close friend now but had been just one of the crowd back in seventh. Rose doubted if she had mentioned Ming in the diary. The same was true of Emma and Caitlin.

She'd written a bit about Jill, a good friend in seventh. But in eighth, where the curriculum was American history, Rose had become fascinated by war. She could not stop reading about battles: half-known Indian conflicts like King Philip's, major battles like Gettysburg. When Jill saw her reading a book about the Civil War, Jill said, "We finished that, you turkey," and when Rose said, "I know, but I'm still excited about it," Jill wandered off, never to return.

Rose imagined the police gathered around a table at this very moment, reading her diary out loud to each other. Were the police laughing at her? Pitying her? Or were they simply bored?

Because how exciting was the life of a seventh grader, after all?

Not very.

Rose flushed with the knowledge that her diary was packed with references to "A." She had spent seventh grade having a crush on Alan Finney, the youngest member of Tabor's band.

Most of Tabor's friends had graduated from high school last year along with Tabor, but Alan Finney was a senior this year. Alan had quite literally never looked at Rose, but Rose had spent a large portion of her life looking at Alan. He was always there to look at, too, being a star in as many sports as Tabor had been.

She imagined the police talking to Alan Finney. *Did you know Rose Lymond worships the ground you walk on?*

Alan would have to stop and think. "Rose?" he would say, puzzled. "You mean Tabor's sister? Come on, gimme a break."

Luckily, the police were investigating a murder, not a seventh-grade crush. They had no way to know that Rose continued to carry the crush around with her.

"Wait up!" shrieked Melinda and Halsey, charging forward to join Ming and Caitlin and Emma and Rose and Richard and Alex and Keith.

Melinda and Halsey had turned sixteen. Halsey had her own car and loved to give rides to people.

I'll probably never have a car and be able to give rides to people, thought Rose. I just stole a car. Mom and Dad are not going to rush me to the Motor Vehicle Bureau for my first license. I might not be driving at sixteen. I might be waiting till I'm twenty-one and in another state.

"I thought we'd never get here," said Halsey. "There was so much traffic this morning."

Traffic.

Rose fell back four years.

Hadn't the police asked about traffic? The roads had been very crowded that weekend. Mr. Lofft exited from the turnpike to go to Frannie Bailey's, whose house was remarkably remote for a place technically just north of the city. He took turn after confusing turn, the house finally revealed between a ravine and a protected marsh.

By the time he and Frannie Bailey finished their shouting match and Mr. Lofft had stomped back to the car, it was five-thirty, and there were still sixty miles to drive. They were in the thick of Friday evening weekend travel and the city streets were maddeningly slow. Mr. Lofft yelled at Anjelica for chomping so loudly on the blue corn chips. Yelled again when Anjelica rolled the crinkly foil up to close the bag.

Biting down on his half-smoked cigar, Mr. Lofft surged forward a few feet as if to drive through the car ahead of him. He swore at people who didn't jump lights and swore at people who did. He yelled at the local government for not planning intersections better and yelled at the world for not giving him his own lane.

They moved ahead two car lengths and the light went red again. He threw the cigar out the window in disgust.

Anjelica whispered, "Don't worry. He's always this upset after he fights with Frannie."

At last, the turnpike entrance lay visible in the distance. Mr. Lofft gunned the engine and they sped under the overhanging branches of big trees, driving half on the grass to pass cars waiting to make left turns, bumping over curbs and gutters, the bulky vehicle feeling as if it might tip; but it didn't, and Mr. Lofft accelerated up the entrance ramp and shot onto the highway at eighty miles an hour.

Rose clung to the seat in front of her but it was Anjelica who cried out. Mr. Lofft swore at his daughter and drove even more erratically. His mood did not improve. He made them turn off the movie. He turned off his book tape and tuned the radio to an all-news AM station. It repeated itself every quarter hour until Rose could lip-synch the headlines.

"Lemme see your botany project," said Richard.

"Huh?" said Rose.

"Your phragmites data," said Richard patiently. "You were going to print it out for me, remember?"

She did not remember agreeing to print out her data. She hardly even remembered Richard.

Rose's love had turned this year from history to science. A botany assignment had changed her life. The teacher was having them experiment with an aggressive swamp weed called *phragmites*: a fifteen-foot-high invader taking over every native marsh. Rose had come up with a root inoculant that crippled but did not destroy her stand of phragmites. She put her mind on swamp reeds but it wouldn't stay.

She found herself having trouble breathing, as if she had asthma. There had been a girl in seventh, known to Rose only by sight, who had actually died of asthma, sitting in the car next to her own mother as they drove to the emergency room, not knowing this attack was worse than any other.

I won't die, Rose reminded herself. Whatever happens to me, my body won't be put in a coffin. But if I talk, life as I know it will die. So this morning, at eleven, I have to face that judge in silence.

She said to Richard, "I'm sorry. I forgot. Give me your e-mail address. I'll send it tonight."

They were with the juvenile judge less than twenty minutes.

Rose again failed to discuss anything.

She did not have to spend a night in any jail. She was not to live at a detention center. They were not going to make her wear an ankle bracelet and be on house arrest. The judge assigned Rose to rehabilitation.

She was to donate fifty hours to her town, picking up trash.

"I hope you're happy," said her mother through tight lips.

Rose said nothing.

CHAPTER FIVE

Rose's great-grandmother still walked a mile every day, although it took her an hour to do it. From May through October, Nannie played croquet when it wasn't raining, whether she had a partner or not. Croquet season had begun, so Wednesday afternoon when Rose came by, Nannie handed her a mallet.

Nannie rattled on about "the girls" she had beaten in bridge last night. Nannie did not lose well. When she was much younger, Rose used to sit in on bridge games, rooting for Nannie. The older Nannie got, the dottier her friends became, and the easier it was to whip them.

In croquet, Rose was yellow. Red was never a choice because Nannie was always red. "I just bought a new computer game. *SlaughterHound III*," Nannie told Rose. "It's so exciting."

"It's violent, is what it is," said Rose, whacking her great-grandmother's ball out of bounds. "You are sick, Nannie."

"Nonsense. Living in New England makes a person stodgy and I have to guard against it. I don't know why I've stayed here eighty-six years. I'm really a California girl. I'm beginning to think I should have handled my life differently."

Rose laughed. "Nannie, you know perfectly well you think you handled your life better than anybody."

Nannie's sharp old eyes pinned Rose. "Better than you."

So Dad had told Nannie. Rose resented it. If nobody at school had to know, why did anybody at home?

"Do you have any violence you'd like to share with me?" said Nannie.

"No."

"You have to talk to somebody, darling."

"I don't, actually. Americans have the right to remain silent."

"I'm your great-grandmother. You don't have silence rights with me."

Rose gave her own yellow ball a tremendous whack, knocking herself into the weeds by the hemlocks. It would take some time, making little baby-size hits, to return to the game. She followed her ball.

Rose had read about contemplative nuns who lived in a cloister and kept silence. They uttered nothing but prayers. Even at dinner, there was no speech.

You really would need convent walls to live that way, because talking was the most important thing in the decade Rose occupied. If you did not talk out loud, you talked by typing into your computer, or you listened to the talk of others, on the radio, the television, or in the chat rooms.

She understood why nuns had worn cowls and wimples. If you were to keep silence, you needed all the protection you could get.

Nannie dropped her mallet on the grass and walked slowly over to one of the cast iron chairs under the weeping willow. She sat down heavily in a chair so encrusted with rust and bird droppings that nobody would get near it.

Wonderful, thought Rose, I've given her a stroke. "Are you all right?" she called.

"No."

Unwillingly, Rose walked back. "Nannie, you know I would suspect you of anything. Are you having a heart attack or is this a ploy to make me talk?"

"It's a ploy, darling. You're so clever. I love that in a person." Nannie patted one of the disgusting chairs. "Sit with me."

Rose sat on the mossy ground instead.

"Rose, darling, your father is my favorite grandson, even though I have four of them. Even though it's wrong to have favorites. And you are my favorite great-grandchild, even though I have eleven. You have my name. I'm Margaret Rose and you're Rose Margaret. I will live on in you."

Nannie's skin was so wrinkled she looked as if life had done to her what Rose had done to the white doughnut bag, spindling and crushing. Standing with a mallet in her hand and the grass beneath her feet, her great-grandmother looked able to go on forever. But collapsed on the ruined chair under the weeping tree, Nannie looked finished. She could die tomorrow.

Rose's throat closed. "Nannie," she said desperately,

"you raised a lot of rim in your day. You've told me a hundred stories about how rowdy you were."

Nannie twined a lock of Rose's hair in her stiff, swollen fingers. Her voice was soft as moss. "Rowdy is fine. Raising rim is fine. But this is criminal, Rose. Your father tells me you were in juvenile court. Oh, honey, it must have been so awful."

Rose could not look into Nannie's face. She dreaded Sunday dinner, when she'd have to look at Mopsy and Popsy. Her grandparents loved to brag about her. Sunday she was expected to run through a list of the week's triumphs in school. She thought of being condemned and cornered by three generations of family.

"You tell me what happened," said Nannie gently. "If I agree that you should stay silent, I'll order your father to stand behind you. I will tell him he's to ask no questions. The family will back you up."

Rose plucked a little mattress of green moss. She used to bring her tiny Fisher Price families out here, building them sod houses with thatch roofs. She changed the subject. "The judge wasn't so bad. My community service is picking up trash along highways. I have to do it for fifty hours."

"That seems excessive."

"I don't mind, Nannie. I thought I'd have to stay in some juvenile detention facility or enter a foster home."

"I'm talking to your father about boarding school," said Nannie.

"Boarding school!" Rose was horrified. "Why would I want to leave home? What about my friends?"

"You'll make new ones. I loved boarding school. I went to Northfield Academy in the Berkshires. Western Massachusetts is beautiful."

"I won't go."

"Rose, Rose," said her great-grandmother. "You are still a child and must do as you are told. Anyway, I don't know how much fun school is going to be from now on. The police are off interrogating your friends as we speak."

Chrissie Klein was astonished to find police standing in her doorway. She was even more astonished to find they wanted to talk about Rose Lymond.

Chrissie could not imagine Rose doing anything wrong. She was a person to be admired, possessing all the virtues, being brave, kind, clean of heart, and honest. This could be annoying. Rose was also careful and deliberate. She didn't think twice before she did something but considered it for six or eight months. This could be *very* annoying.

Both officers were hung with weapons and badges, trousers crisply ironed and bodies solid. The woman's name tag said Megan Moran. She was over six feet tall. How she must have intimidated Rose, who was only five five. For the millionth time, Chrissie dreamed of being taller, because in basketball, Chrissie's five ten was pitiful. "Bet you played basketball," she said to Megan Moran.

"Yup. St. Mary's High. Then Boston. But I didn't last. I wasn't good enough."

Chrissie planned to die before thinking, let alone saying out loud, "I wasn't good enough."

"Are your parents home, Chrissie? We'd like them to be present."

"Come on in. My mother's here." Chrissie's heart sank. Mom was an adolescent psychologist. She believed every teenage girl should want to be admired for her mind and spirit. Chrissie wanted to be admired for her body. This caused arguments.

The moment her mother was here, everything would become complex, with extra meaning and tiresome layers. On the other hand, Mom would not let the police get away with one molecule of pressure, and that was good.

"Mom," she called.

Just as it was important for Chrissie to look wonderful, it was important to her mother to attach no meaning to looks. Mom wore a sagging, faded black dress, white athletic socks with dark shoes, and no makeup. Her glasses had had the same frames for half Chrissie's life. She had not yet fixed her speckled black-and-gray hair. She looked vaguely like a porcupine, bristling with quills, ready to pierce passing police officers.

"You will recall the murder of Frannie Bailey almost four years ago," said Megan Moran. "Frannie Bailey was the partner of Milton Lofft. The murder probably took place on Friday of the weekend Rose Lymond visited the Lofft estate."

How envious Chrissie had been. All that glamour and wealth — and it was Rose who snagged the weekend. Chrissie had angled for a friendship with Anjelica but never achieved it.

"On that Friday afternoon," said Megan Moran, "Milton and Anjelica Lofft picked Rose up. Mr. Lofft stopped en route at his partner's house. We believed then and we believe now that Milton Lofft murdered his partner while his daughter and Rose sat waiting in the car. No charges were brought because the physical evidence was weak. But the case has been reopened."

Wow, thought Chrissie, I wonder why. DNA evidence, which they might not have had before? Some secret witness?

She began to feel the same sick fascination with the crime that had gripped her four years ago. She'd had high hopes that Rose had seen it happen and would be a vital witness at the trial, which would be televised, so Chrissie could stay up late to watch attorney experts on TV analyze Rose's words.

"Day before yesterday, we questioned Rose again," said Megan Moran. "Again Rose claimed to remember nothing. On the off chance that Rose had written down some long-forgotten clue, Mrs. Lymond gave us a diary Rose kept that year. It was put in the police car to be read later. To prevent us from reading the diary, Rose stole the police car, drove to Burger King, went into the rest room, ripped up the murder weekend pages, and flushed the shreds away. Then she waved us down to arrest her."

"Awesome!" Chrissie couldn't help laughing and cheering. She imagined Rose, in her cautious way, signaling early and often — in a stolen police car. Rose would be a goddess at school. "You do not know how out of character that is. I cannot wait to tease her."

Mrs. Klein was not pleased with her daughter's reaction. She said stiffly to the police, "You cannot conclude from her reluctance to have her diary examined that Rose witnessed anything. Little girls write things they later regret. Perhaps she was repeating vicious gossip or discussing her sexual yearnings."

Chrissie cringed. She detested having a mother who talked like that. Rose would detest it even more.

Megan Moran shook her head. "We think she's protecting Milton Lofft."

What happened to you when you stole a police car? Would Rose go to jail? That would not be awesome at all. Chrissie would be a character witness; explain that stealing a police car was an aberration. Perhaps Rose had been on something. Except Rose was not the type to be on anything other than an academic high.

"Mrs. Lymond keeps a detailed family date book," said Megan Moran, "and she doesn't throw them out but saves them the way other people save photo albums. She dug out that year's calendar for us. We discovered that Rose had a slumber party the following weekend. Erin, Halsey, Jill, Melinda, and you, Chrissie, were invited."

Shock ripped through Chrissie Klein.

She should have known instantly what this was about. How could she have forgotten one word? But four years was a quarter of her life. Time enough to fill her mind with other things.

"What do you remember about that slumber party, Chrissie?" asked the policewoman.

Chrissie shrugged helplessly, although she despised helpless people, especially girls.

"Surely a bunch of girls jammed in the same bedroom and giggling into the night begged for details about a murder. Surely you, her friends, pressed Rose very hard."

"We begged," agreed Chrissie. "We offered bribes of friendship and chocolate. But Rose said it had been boring and there was nothing to tell and we couldn't believe it."

Chrissie especially had not believed it. Not for one minute.

Mrs. Lymond had probably not entered it in her date book, because it was a constant, but Tabor's band had been practicing in the basement. The seventh-grade girls adored the older boys. Rose's special crush was on Alan Finney. Chrissie herself worshiped whichever boy bothered to say hello. Jill and Melinda were in love with Tabor. Halsey and Erin loved to watch Verne Burnett, the oldest in the band and the one most likely to practice with his shirt off.

And so when Rose suggested going down to the basement to see if the boys would play Ping-Pong or pool with them (which they wouldn't, because fifteen- and sixteen-year-old boys were nauseated by the presence of twelve-year-old girls), everybody stormed down two sets of stairs, their hopes high and their hair fixed.

Except Chrissie, who stayed behind to read Rose's diary.

Rose's bed had a big slanted wooden headboard with a lock. When you threw all the pillows on the floor, you could spot the half-hidden keyhole, and if you went into Rose's closet and lifted her bathrobe from its hook, you found the key. Inside the headboard were cubbies, poorly designed and hard to get at. Rose kept her diary at the bottom of the left-hand cubby.

Chrissie remembered the texture of the leather cover. The gleam of the gold-rimmed pages. She remembered flipping quickly to the end, reading with hot, eager eyes. The entries stunned and horrified her. She read them a second time, slowly, as if expecting a nicer, better version on the second try. Then she chucked the diary back into the cubby and slammed the wooden lid, fumbling badly with the key.

She thundered downstairs to catch up with the others, pretending she'd been in the bathroom. She arrived just as the boys yelled at them to beat it. Halsey and Erin were complaining because Verne wasn't around that night and she remembered thinking what a tiny complaint that was, compared to what Rose had on her mind. She wondered how Rose could bear to have them in the house. She wondered how Rose could bear anything.

And yet, Chrissie had forgotten.

"Why wouldn't Anjelica have been invited?" asked the policewoman.

Chrissie surfaced with difficulty. "The party probably wasn't good enough for Anjelica," she said. "She went through friends like a recycler through aluminum cans."

Immediately she was ashamed. You shouldn't hold against somebody how she'd behaved in seventh grade. "Listen," she corrected herself, "we barely knew Anjelica. We were just in class together. She was new when school started the last week in August and she moved away before Thanksgiving. I haven't thought of her for years and I don't think Rose has, either."

Oh, Rose! she thought. You might forgive me for invading your privacy and going into your cubby and reading your diary. You probably wouldn't even be surprised, because what seventh graders are is untrustworthy, snoopy, and mean. But you would never forgive me for knowing the truth. I can't even pick up the phone to tell you I'm on your team. You were alone then and you have to do this alone now.

"We need your help, Chrissie," said Megan Moran. "If Rose is protecting a killer, that killer will be scared right now. He needs her silence. He might decide he can't trust her silence. He might decide to silence her forever."

But Chrissie Klein, too, said nothing.

• • •

Alan Finney was home when the police arrived, which was rare for Alan, since he played sports year-round and when he wasn't at practice, worked at a garden center. He liked lifting bales of hay, sacks of bird-seed, pallets of cobblestones, and trees whose root balls weighed as much as the customer. He'd inherited the job from Verne, a guy in Tabor's band, whose brains the owner had compared to a tree stump. For months at the nursery, Alan got compliments for no reason except he wasn't Verne.

Alan had dumped his sports equipment and books and snacks and computer stuff on the floor of the front hall, which was his basic exchange system. His parents used the side door so as to avoid breaking an ankle.

The police made no comment as they forded the stream of Alan's possessions and made it into the living room. The living room was even worse, because his sister was getting married, and wedding plans and pos-sibilities were strewn on every surface. They talked standing up.

The policewoman was his own height, six one. He studied her name tag. "Did you play for St. Mary's?"

She was extremely pleased to be recognized.

"My sister went to St. Mary's," Alan explained.

"Hey? Would that be Cecily Finney?" said the po-licewoman, beaming. "Say hi to her for me. Is this her wedding you're planning?"

"*I'm* not planning it," said Alan with a shudder.

When they started talking about Rose Lymond, Alan was simply astonished. If there was a person more law-abiding, more cautious, more academic, Alan hadn't met her. She was such a contrast to Tabor, who was not all that law-abiding, never cautious, and despised academics. It was actually kind of a miracle that any college had taken Tabor. Of course, he had had to go two thousand miles to find one.

"*Stole a police car?*" said Alan. "*Rose?* Impossible. A definite case of mistaken identity."

The police explained why there was no mistake about it.

Alan couldn't imagine Rose stealing a paper clip. "But why?" he said. He didn't tell the two police that he thought Rose had done something outrageously wonderful. Or insane.

Craig Gretzak told him about the diary and its place in the murder investigation.

A few months ago, when Alan turned eighteen, the baseball coach had coaxed most of the team to donate blood. Alan had not done well at the sight of needles. His head and heart and knees blended, and he found himself on the floor, with a doctor saying, "Alan, you better not try this again. You are literally green."

I'm probably green now, he thought.

He managed to stay upright, though, which he had not accomplished at the Red Cross. He busied himself shifting wedding stuff onto the floor so they could sit on the couch. Cecily's magazines seemed harder to lift than a pallet of patio slate.

"We retrieved the remains of the diary," said Craig Gretzak, "and we're talking to any kid Rose mentions. Mrs. Lymond helped us interpret some of the entries. It looks as if you know the Lymonds well."

"Just Tabor." Tabor had the largest family Alan had ever come across: uncles, aunts, cousins, grandparents, great-grandparents. He was always visiting or being visited by some relative or other. By high school, Tabor was embarrassed by so much family and spent much time in seclusion, hoping to avoid them. "Why can't I be an orphan?" Tabor moaned. "Why can't I be normal and have all my relatives living in other states, with mountain ranges between us?"

A rock band had created something of a mountain range. No relatives visited when the band was practicing. Now that Alan was eighteen he could admit none of them had had talent. But they had sure had fun.

Nobody in the band paid any attention to Tabor's kid sister. It was pesky the way she'd sit on the top step of the basement stairs writing away in her diary when the band rehearsed below. "Beat it, Rose," Tabor would yell.

"No. These are my stairs, too."

"Well, cut it out with the journal. Stop writing about us."

"Why would I write about you?"

"Because we're interesting and you're not."

Regular brother and sister stuff. Exactly the way Alan talked to his sister. Eventually Tabor would reduce Rose to tears and she'd leave.

"Where does she keep the diary?" Verne asked once. Verne had started the group but proved to be incapable of memorizing two chords in a row. Verne's idea of practice was to be on the phone ordering pizzas. But he'd had his driver's license and an old Volvo wagon into which they managed to fit drums, speakers, wires, cord, keyboard, and band members. Alan, the youngest, had been forced to sit with the drinks cooler under his feet and two guitar cases wedged under his chin.

Tabor shrugged, not because he didn't know where Rose kept her diary but because he didn't care. "In the headboard of her bed," he said. "She keeps the key on the hook behind her bathrobe and thinks nobody knows."

"Let's steal the diary," Verne suggested.

It was at that moment that Tabor became the leader of the group and not Verne. "That would make us twelve years old, too," Tabor said. "That's what little boys do — torment little girls. We're trying to be musicians here, Verne. Although it's a struggle for you. Okay, everybody, take it from the top."

One day, Tabor actually mentioned his sister. She was going to visit the Loffts for a weekend. They had all been impressed. The Loffts were exciting people and Anjelica seemed much older than twelve. The boys discussed what Anjelica's figure would be in a few more years. Nobody cared what Rose's figure would be.

The weekend was chaotic. Musically, the band

changed forever when Verne called up to say he was quitting because he had better things to do. They not only had to find another musician, they had to find other transportation. Furthermore, Alan had had a major paper due and had to stay up all Sunday night to pull it off. He slept through class Monday, ended up in the principal's office to discuss whether he had a drug problem, and Monday night heard about the murder of Milton Lofft's partner. By Tuesday it was known that Milton Lofft had been the last person to see the victim alive.

Tabor called practice on Wednesday and the entire band happened to be in the cellar while the police interrogated Rose. Well, except for Verne, who never did come back. Alan still thought it was unprofessional of him.

Rose, who could write five pages sitting on the top step watching the band, could not come up with one sentence about an entire weekend with the Loffts. The band knew because they were standing on the pool table with their ears literally pressed to the ceiling, trying to hear every word spoken in the room above.

"But what about —?" said the police, "and how about —?"

"Nothing," said Rose.

"I can't remember," said Rose.

"I didn't see," said Rose.

Tabor was embarrassed. Everybody had been hoping to get in on hot police activity and glamorous crime, and his sister was a complete dud. They played softly, so Mr. Lymond wouldn't come to the top of the stairs and yell at them and so they could get over their embarrassment at having listened in to start with.

Alan's fingers moved automatically on his keyboard while his mind fixed on Rose. She's so smart, he thought. Much smarter than Tabor. Twice as smart as me. Smart enough to have seen and understood everything. Her brother believes her lame little statements. I don't.

A few nights later, during band practice, Alan ran upstairs to the kitchen for a cold soda. Rose was standing in the middle of the room doing nothing, holding nothing, and as far he could tell, seeing nothing. "Hey, Rose," he said cheerfully. "No diary tonight?"

Her head snapped back as if he had struck her. He actually looked down at his hand to see if he'd done that, and then looked at her cheek to see if it was bruised.

She was not breathing. Her entire body, including her eyes, was rigid. It was like a motionless seizure. "You okay, Rose?" he said uncertainly.

Her body turned in his direction. A few beats later she looked in his direction. She still had not blinked. "I outgrew keeping a diary," she said. She backed away from him.

Outgrew it when? thought Alan. Last Thursday you were sitting on the cellar steps, scribbling away.

Rose fled from the kitchen. She literally ran away

from him. The sensation of having slapped her lived on in the flat of Alan's hand and the muscles of his arm.

You may have stopped *writing* in a diary, thought Alan, but I bet you didn't stop *keeping* it. I bet you still have it. And you wouldn't have a silent seizure unless you had a serious secret written down in that diary.

It was only an hour before Mr. and Mrs. Lymond and Rose drove off to visit relatives and the rest of the band drove off to pick up pizzas. Alan claimed he wasn't in the mood to get off the couch. He stayed by himself in the basement.

How silent was this house that usually rocked with percussion. He could hear newly made ice cubes clunking inside the refrigerator. A clock ticking.

Alan walked upstairs. He entered Rose's room. The key was where Tabor said it would be. Against the slanted wooden headboard of Rose's large bed were a dozen frothy pillows. He imagined slumber parties, with girls leaning on pillows to eat and giggle and watch TV. He shifted the pillows carefully so he could put them back in order. His fingers scrounged around the cubby, closing on a leather book as pretty as any volume he had ever touched.

How well he remembered Rose's handwriting, the graceful slope of each letter. He remembered the final pages where her handwriting disintegrated into a frantic blotchy scrawl. Over and around the words he read in such shock were odd puckered circles.

Dried tears.

In his remembering, Alan forgot the present. Now it returned in the voice of a cop. "We're wondering, Alan," said Craig Gretzak softly, "if Rose saw something else that weekend. Nothing to do with Milton Lofft. Something to do with Tabor. Or you."

CHAPTER SIX

It was now Thursday.

Rose's father drove her to school. Her parents were rarely willing to drive her, since there was a perfectly good bus, and anyhow, it cramped their work schedules. But Rose's father was afraid of her choices now. For all he knew, a daughter who stole a car at the beginning of the week might be headed toward drugs and prostitution by the end of the week. Rose had thought of her silence as a way to keep the family together, not tear it apart. "Bye, Dad," she said softly.

He tried to smile, but nothing came of it. He actually seemed more gray and more lined in only a few days. He was certainly more upset than she had ever seen him. Mom, too, was raw and frayed at the edges. Even Tabor's shenanigans had not disturbed her parents like this, perhaps because they saw Tabor's actions as nonsense, whereas they had expected Rose to grow up neatly and without bringing pain to their hearts.

She had not yet shut the car door when Augusta spotted her, flung her own book bag down, and leaped like a crazy woman to greet Rose.

Rose liked Augusta enormously and would have

liked to be closer friends, but Augusta always seemed to be with somebody else or interested in something different. Rose had not actually been around Augusta since fourth grade, when the teacher fixed their little desks in sets of four, facing in, and Augusta had sat directly opposite Rose.

"It cannot be true," said Augusta, plowing to a halt. "Science project star, history-loving, never-swearing Rose Margaret Lymond? Stealing police cars?"

If Augusta knew, everybody knew. Rose smiled at Augusta out of leftover fourth-grade memory. "Actually, just one police car," she said. She shut the car door and walked off without looking back to see how Augusta's greeting had played with her father. Oh, Daddy, she thought. I'm doing this for you, and you'll never know, and I can never let you know.

Augusta fell into step with her. They ignored the long, slanted ramp and took the steep stairs. Quietly and seriously Augusta said, "Do you need help, Rose? I don't know what's happening, and I'm not asking, but there must be something radically wrong. Your father looks terrible. Rose, if you need me, I'm your friend."

People who hardly knew him could tell that this was destroying her father. "Thank you, Gussie." She ignored the tremor in her voice, hoping Augusta would be kind enough to ignore it, too. "I think everything will work out."

Augusta nodded without saying more and Rose wondered whether she had crushed or opened a future friendship with Augusta. But there was no time to continue the conversation. Ming arrived. "Is it true?" she demanded.

"Is what true?"

"Rose! Don't be difficult. That you stole a police car, of course."

"Oh. That. Yes. It's true."

Ming howled with delight. "Tell me exactly what happened."

"And me," said Emma.

"And us," said Caitlin and Halsey and Richard and Keith and Alex, grinning and waiting.

They seemed to find Rose and her car theft rather cute. They seemed, in fact, to regard her as an episode in a good TV show. Only Augusta realized that there must be something very wrong.

"Come on, tell us!" cried Ming.

I can hardly say I don't remember, thought Rose. It was this week. If I say, "It's a long story," they'll be twice as happy and settle in for all the details. "It's under litigation," she said finally. "I can't talk about it."

"Bosh. Rot. Balderdash," said Ming.

Everybody laughed.

Rose tried to walk toward class but they were clinging to her. It was like walking through a department store, brushed by clothing displays and countertops.

"Come on, really," coaxed Ming.

Rose was saved by, of all people, the principal's secretary. Dr. Siegal and Mr. Burgess wished to see Miss Lymond, said the secretary.

Last week, her friends would have assumed Rose was being summoned because she had won a prize, placed in some essay contest, was sought after by the university for her phragmites data. They'd have been bored. But now that Rose was in trouble — lots of trouble, oceans of trouble — they were delighted.

Why had Rose not realized how much attention stealing a cop car would bring?

It was funny, in a dreadful way. You spent your whole life trying to attract attention, trying to be interesting and pretty and smart and graceful and wanted. Then you got the attention and it was like being hit over the head with a baseball bat.

First period bells rang.

Reluctantly the crowd around her dispersed and went on to class. Ming was slow to depart. She gave Rose plenty of time to say, Of course I'll tell *you*; *you're* my best friend; I wouldn't leave *you* out.

Rose did not say it.

She could see no point in hurrying to meet with the principal and vice principal. She walked so slowly that both men had appeared in the office doorway by the time she finally arrived. Star students always got to know the administration. She liked the two men well enough, although they were pompous and played favorites.

She did not go into the office. "I expect you have received a report from the police," she said courteously. "This is a delicate family situation. I cannot discuss it with you. It has nothing to do with school and I do not want to be late for botany."

"Rose, we're so concerned. Come into the office and share with us," said Mr. Burgess.

I don't share well, thought Rose. I think we established that when I refused to share my diary. And if I'm not going to share with Dad or Mom or poor old doing-her-job Megan Moran, I'm unlikely to share with you two. "You're welcome to talk to the judge," she said politely.

"You're a juvenile. He won't talk to us," said Dr. Siegal grumpily.

Rose kept her voice so courteous she sounded like Nannie in an earlier century. "I'm afraid I will have to follow the same rule. Please excuse me." She turned stiffly like a doll made from a wooden spoon and neither of them intercepted her.

Ignoring two principals turned out to be rather like stealing a police car.

Do it quickly and cleanly. It's over before they can stop you.

On her way to botany, Rose happened to pass the library. She walked in and tapped a few keywords on the nearest computer screen. There actually was a book on the subject that concerned her: Dewey decimal number 070, a shelf in the library where Rose had never gone. She preferred 500s — biology, botany; or 973 — American history.

The book was in, of course; who would check it out?

Rose browsed through a history of diary writing.

Five million diaries were sold every year in America, which seemed like enough. How surprising that even with e-mail and handheld computers and laptops and computer disks and instant messaging, people were still sitting down and laboriously scribbling in paper books.

Diaries were a rather recent concept, the book said. For most of literate time, people didn't think of writing about themselves every day. Then, in the sixteenth century, ministers began to keep daily track of whether they had been pure of thought.

Why did I write? wondered Rose.

I wanted to be sure Grandfather and Nannie knew what a nice present they'd given me. So I wrote to be polite.

I wrote because I loved my handwriting. I loved the shape of my letters and the way I dotted my i's with a circle.

I wrote because I felt important. I, Rose Margaret Lymond, would be a red leather book with gold edges.

The question is not why I wrote it. It's why I kept it.

It was Alan Finney, not Ming, who met Rose at her locker after school. Their paths did not usually overlap. He had had to search her out.

Her pulse skyrocketed. I still adore him, she thought. She could not manage an attractive, relaxed smile. Her lips stretched as if she were wearing braces that had just been tightened. Immediately she wondered about her hair.

Alan took a deep breath. He looked around to make sure nobody could overhear. He was so furtive that several people stopped in their tracks to see what he was up to. He said, "The police talked to me, Rose."

Her cheeks went hot and scarlet. She began turning the dial on the combination lock, gradually realizing she was facing the wrong locker.

"They told me you stole that police car to buy yourself time to destroy the diary."

Rose shrugged. But she remembered that moment in the kitchen, a week or so after the murder, when Alan noticed she wasn't writing in her diary anymore. Not one other person had ever commented on that.

Alan seemed at a loss for what to say next. He breathed heavily in and out. Rose felt the same. "They asked how well I knew you," said Alan. "I said the way any guy knows his friend's little sister. Not very well."

She shrugged again, though it hurt.

"I've never seen you shrug," said Alan after a while. "It's not your style."

"I don't have a style."

"Of course you do. You're dignified and reserved and careful."

Rose nearly groaned out loud. She had never heard three more ghastly adjectives. That was how a handsome, wonderful, sexy boy perceived her? Dignified, reserved, and careful? She wanted to rip off her skin and start over.

Alan said, "I'd help if I could, Rose."

"Help the police?" she said, feeling even more exhausted.

Alan said something extremely rude about the police. "Help you," he explained.

She almost smiled. Wouldn't Augusta and Alan be a nice pair of helpers?

Alan slouched against the lockers, his height and breadth blocking her from all gazes. He was a foot taller than she was. She knew, because the stats on every player were published. "Tabor called me," said Alan, and in spite of herself, Rose was deflated. So after all this time, the loving big brother had finally kicked in.

"He's worried," said Alan. "And jealous, I think. His little sister is the one with the guts to steal a police car. Any trouble Tabor ever got into just became minor league. You're the one playing in the majors."

Rose managed a smile, but she did not manage to direct it at Alan. She was facing the metal louvers of somebody else's locker, as if it were a mirror and she were trying on lipstick.

"Rose, you can't even look at *me*. How are you going to look at police and attorneys putting pressure on you?"

He could not know that police and attorneys were easier to look at than he was. At least the police had given Alan no idea of her crush. He didn't know that all through those casual music-rehearsal hours, a little girl's hopes had soared whenever he said hello. She sighed inwardly and looked up. But Alan Finney's face held no worried concern like Augusta's, no hot fascination like Ming's, no frustrated ignorance like the principals'. There was no resigned obedience to the wishes of his friend Tabor. In Alan's eyes was an intensity of emotion Rose had not expected and could not interpret. Helplessly they watched each other flush.

Maybe he's just embarrassed, thought Rose. All kinds of people are seeing us together and he hates the conclusions they're drawing and he's just waiting for this to end. "Did the police show you the diary?" she said, as if it hardly mattered.

"No. I think they're talking to everybody whose name you mentioned in the pages they still have. They're hoping you shared your experiences with one of us after the murder."

"I didn't have any experiences to share," said Rose. "It's very thoughtful of you to be concerned, Alan." Even though Tabor ordered you to be, she thought. "But this will come to an end shortly, when the authorities accept that I cannot contribute to their pile of evidence."

Alan drew a breath so deep that his ribs banged into the tops of the lockers on one side and his book bag swung out into the traffic of the hallway on the other. "Listen, how about going for a Coke with me, Rose? We can talk. I feel as if you need a friend, and I know your family so well — and — you know."

She had hoped for this for half of her life. But what

would she say when he brought up the sole topic of interest? *This is private, Alan. It doesn't involve you.* That contained a clue and she could not give clues to anybody. Alan would phone Tabor and quote her. With a shock, she realized that she had given the two principals a clue. They didn't hear it, she told herself. They won't remember it. "Thank you, Alan, but I have community service. I'm on my way to the corner right now to get picked up by the transport van." Tell him you'll go out with him another time, she ordered herself. Tell him —

But she didn't.

"You of all people," said Alan. "I can't stand the thought of the creeps you'll be with. What will you actually be doing?"

"Picking up trash along highways."

"Really? What highway?"

"Wherever the van drops me, I guess." She had to extricate herself from this before she flung herself against his chest and begged him to go with her. "I'm late, Alan, thanks for, umm, you know, being so nice. See you. Bye."

She walked away from him before he could walk away from her, but there was no safety in any direction. Ming had been watching the whole thing from down the corridor.

"He asked you out and you said no?" hissed Ming when Rose had nowhere to go except up to her.

"He didn't actually ask me out. He promised Tabor he'd —" Rose stopped. She didn't have the energy for this.

"Oh, well. Let's go to my house," said Ming. "My parents don't get home from work till six-thirty. You and I can really talk because it'll be absolutely private and you can tell me everything."

"There isn't anything to tell, Ming. Anyway, I can't go to your house today because I have community service. I'm picking up trash on roadways. It sounds kind of interesting. You wear these orange —"

"I don't care what you wear to pick up trash," snapped Ming. "And don't pretend you don't remember taking the police car. What are you going to plead? Memory loss? Insanity? You remember every detail of it, Rose, and you know it."

Oddly enough, Rose did not remember every detail. In fact the details, both now and four years ago, had evaporated quickly.

How grateful she had been for seventh grade after her Lofft visit weekend, because school was as filling as doughnuts. By the end of any school day, Rose felt entirely full, heavy in her stomach, as if she'd eaten an entire dozen.

Only weeks later, Christmas of her seventh grade, somebody gave Dad a telescope, on the theory that he wanted to watch hawks soaring in the sky. "What did I ever say to make anybody think that?" Dad mumbled. He set the telescope by the bay window, and there it gathered dust. Now and then, Rose would focus on a distant tree or roof.

For four years, she had seen her mother and father as if through that scope. Close up and painfully clear.

Then they would slide out of view, and finding them again was difficult.

Yet as the weeks and months passed, Rose actually forgot.

Every now and then some phrase or glance would hit her in the face. Rose would want to sink to her knees and cry out, but she would force herself to think of Nannie. No matter how steep the stairs, Nannie labored up and down. No matter how stiff her knees, Nannie gripped that racket. No matter how painful her fingers, Nannie played the piano. So no matter how stiff Rose's heart, she must keep going.

"Have you written me off?" said Ming fiercely. "I'm not good enough to tell things to? I'm the last one to find out that you've started stealing vehicles, going to judges, getting probation, and having your friends interrogated?"

"I'm sorry, Ming, but I can't be late. The judge —"

"They didn't come to *my* house, of course. I guess they only interviewed the important people in your life."

If she did not get out of here soon, Rose was going to lie down on the floor and assume fetal position. "I'm sorry, Ming," said Rose, who was.

They lived in an age where passing information was the most important thing on the planet. People spent their lives in the exchange of knowledge. If something happened, everybody deserved to know. Some people deserved to know first.

Rose had broken the rule with her best friend.

Ming stalked away.

Alone at last, Rose walked out of the high school. Far across the student parking lot, she saw Chrissie Klein waving and starting to run toward her. If the police had talked to Alan, they had talked to Chrissie. Rose fled, running all the way to the intersection where the transport van waited.

CHAPTER SEVEN

$\int$ even people were being rehabilitated along with Rose: two teenage boys and five men, all of whom claimed to have drinking problems, now solved.

Everybody assumed that Rose also had a drinking problem.

The only thing Rose had ever drunk to excess was iced tea, when she was about eight, and she and Chrissie decided to see how much they could drink before they popped. She could remember (thankfully, long before her diary days, so there was no record) being unable to hop up and down, her legs were so tightly crossed, while Chrissie panted, "My bladder's bigger than your bladder."

"I won't drink again," said the men in childlike voices, as they were given big shiny orange traffic vests. Each vest was padded like a flotation device, as if they might be diving for trash underwater. The heavy-duty gloves were so large that Rose's hands fit into the palm part. Each of them was given a long wooden stick like a broom handle, but with a nail tip, to spear disgusting stuff.

"I've quit drinking," said each man, aghast that he was to be placed on a roadside in public, as if he had done something wrong. Everybody but Rose had a baseball-style cap to yank down over his forehead and hide his face. Everybody told Rose to keep her back to traffic, instead of facing it, or else somebody might recognize her.

"Don't you have to be facing the traffic in order to jump out of the way?" asked Rose.

"You're not gonna be in the road," said the supervisor. "You're gonna keep the traffic barrier between you and the cars. Don't step over it. There's no garbage worth dying for."

In the van, the men embarked on long, sad stories of alcohol hazes and how they had put the past forever behind them. Rose, who could not put the past behind her, envied them. She clung to her roll of plastic bags and ties.

"Forget the cigarette butts and the really little stuff," said the supervisor. "You're after bottles, cans, plastic bags, Styrofoam, broken suitcases, whatever."

Each person was dropped off half a mile apart on the northbound side of Interstate 395. The van would circle, making sure nobody was dropping from heat exhaustion, or running out of drinking water, or trying to leave town.

She did not make eye contact with the teenage boys. What if she liked one of them? What could be worse than finding your first boyfriend at the side of the road during trash detail? Sharing a romantic moment of Styrofoam-stabbing?

But one of them nudged her. "Wanna wear my

cap?" He was disfigured by acne and crooked teeth, but his smile was kind. He said softly, "Mostly the cars is going by so fast they don't see you at all. Nobody's gonna know you. But under the cap you can sort of hide out. You could stick your hair under this."

Rose's blond hair was shoulder length. It was thin and she rarely wore it in a ponytail because she looked bald. Rose needed all the hair she could get and liked it right up next to her face. He was offering her an old minor league baseball cap, black with a red machine-embroidered logo and a misshapen bill from going through the wash.

"Thank you," she said. She tucked her hair inside and jammed the bill down on her forehead. The van pulled into the wide right-hand breakdown lane. Rose got out and stepped over the thigh-high metal guardrail and onto the grass, and the van drove away.

A wide, low hill had been sliced through the middle by the Interstate, two lanes in each direction lying in a shady valley between two long, grassy slopes. The north- and southbound lanes were divided by a football field of grass. Rose was on the northbound side.

A half mile of highway turned out to have a lot of garbage. There was a tire and tire shreds, two hubcaps, an alarm clock, and several hundred brightly colored advertising inserts that had lost their way. There were dirty napkins, half a paperback book, and a rotting T-shirt.

Rose filled a bag and rolled the tire over next to it,

wondering how the tire had managed to get across the guardrail.

The sun was pleasantly warm and the road surprisingly interesting.

She glanced up now and then, checking out dragging mufflers or radios loud enough to be heard in the next county. She scrambled up the grassy hill to fetch Styrofoam or used Pampers, but mostly she stood in knee-high green grass, flecked here and there with early white daisies or poison ivy, reaching in for plastic water bottles and paper coffee cups.

This was the most unlikely after-school activity Rose Lymond ever expected to take up.

Every now and then, a vehicle strayed slightly out of its lane, its right tires running over the cut marks in the emergency lane designed to wake them up. The noise was shocking, like a sudden freight train, ending the instant the car corrected its wheels. Rose decided it was better not to look at the traffic. Sturdy as the protective metal fence was, Rose could not believe it would really hold back a truck going eighty miles an hour.

The wind rushed down the cupped valley, yanking the baseball cap from her head and lifting her blond hair. For a moment she felt beautiful, like a model in a shampoo commercial. She laughed out loud. Models hardly ever wore padded orange trash vests.

The laugh healed her a little. She straightened up, with such a crick in her spine she felt like Nannie.

So many cars coming so fast. Even now hundreds of

them were probably rolling their windows down, preparing to chuck trash into her half mile. Way up ahead she could see a fellow worker on his hillside. The man south of her had not yet come over his hill but a dark SUV, like a square barrel on high tires, had paused in the emergency lane, blinkers on. Once she would have assumed the driver was checking his map. Now she knew he was getting rid of pizza crusts and old shoes.

Her grassy field came to an end, sloping down sharply to a narrow local road that passed beneath the Interstate. The road was so little used there wasn't even a line painted down the middle. To reach the rest of her half mile, Rose would have to climb over the guardrail and walk on the overpass for a hundred feet. Oh, well, the emergency lane was designed so that fire engines and ambulances could pass on the right. There was plenty of room for one thin girl, even in a padded vest.

The lost baseball cap, tossed brutally in the wind tunnels of each passing car, came to rest in the center of the overpass. It huddled up against the cement curb along with lots of other trash.

The guardrail was nearly as high as her waist. Awkwardly she crossed over, lifting her spear so she didn't put it through her foot. The cap was blowing around again. She hoped it wouldn't be whisked out of reach. She heard the rumble of tires on the cut marks, but she was used to the racket now and turned without much interest.

A car was halfway out of its lane, hurtling forward on the diagonal across the emergency lane.

It was not braking.

It was going to hit the bridge.

It would hit Rose first.

Chrissie Klein had not had time for breakfast before she left for school, so she was having it after school. Chrissie was a big refined-sugar fan. She was having a Pop-Tart, a sight from which her mother had to be protected, as she did not approve of white sugar. As soon as she finished the Pop-Tart, Chrissie planned to have Froot Loops.

The Kleins had many phone lines: Chrissie's, her mother's office, her father's office, the fax, and the dedicated Internet. When her own phone rang, Chrissie spoke into it with her mouth full, not worried because any friend of Chrissie's would have equally low standards of phone etiquette. "Yeah, hello?" she said.

"Chrissie, it's Anjelica Lofft."

The Pop-Tart all but fell out of Chrissie's mouth. "Anjelica?" she repeated stupidly. "Lofft?"

"Yes. How are you, Chrissie?"

Sugar and crumbs stuck to her tongue and throat. She felt choky and anxious.

"May we talk?" said Anjelica.

Chrissie loved to talk. Talking was the reason for life. The problem with school was that during those forty-five-minute stretches of class, only the teacher was supposed to talk. Chrissie had never been able to cope with that. She could think of a million things to ask Anjelica. "Well? Did he murder her? Were you there? Did you see? How's boarding school? Do you like being a zillionaire? Want to share a million or two?"

But what came out of her mouth was, "You never invited me for a weekend." Chrissie was humiliated and astonished to hear herself say that out loud. Four years later she was still so crushed that she actually admitted it? Yikes, thought Chrissie. Time for self-improvement.

"If we hadn't moved away, I would have," said Anjelica. "I was envious of the close friendship you had with Rose."

Rose, thought Chrissie. This is about Rose. How strange.

"The nightmare is back," said Anjelica. "Once again, the police are convinced that my father murdered his partner. They are equally convinced Rose saw it happen. Rose could not have seen it happen because it didn't happen. Rose and I saw exactly the same thing because we were waiting in exactly the same car at exactly the same time."

"So why aren't you calling Rose?" asked Chrissie.

"I thought she might have discussed something with you."

"Rose is a very closemouthed person."

"I guess so. I heard about the police-car stunt."

It wasn't a stunt, thought Chrissie. It was an unavoidable act of courage. But that was most certainly not the business of snippy snobby Anjelica Lofft, so Chrissie said, "How could you possibly know what Rose

Lymond is doing in her spare time in a town you haven't visited in years?"

"We're living at the lake estate again," said Anjelica. "We're only ninety miles north."

But the car theft hadn't been on the news or in the papers. Rose's astonishing act had become common knowledge only when the police questioned the diary names, and Halsey and Jill and Erin had been up half the night on e-mail and phone, making sure everybody knew. But the "everybody" they notified were kids in school. How could Anjelica know? With whom was she still friends?

"The police were *here*," said Anjelica, as if the very soil on her property would have to be cleaned now.

Chrissie frowned.

The police were hoping to arrest Mr. Lofft for murder. Why tell him about Rose? Shouldn't they be a little more protective of somebody they wanted as their star witness? This did not sound protective of Rose. It sounded protective of Milton Lofft.

"What did Rose tell you about her weekend with me back when it happened?" asked Anjelica.

Chrissie reverted to seventh-grade behavior. "That you were barely polite, hadn't arranged a single activity, and didn't even sleep in the same room."

"That's true," said Anjelica. "I think we had other things on our minds."

"*We?*" repeated Chrissie Klein. "You and your father? Like, what could have been on your little mind,

Anjelica? Murder?" she said cruelly, remembering the pleasure of finding out, as all seventh graders did, how easily you could hurt somebody. Power was when you slashed somebody down.

Anjelica hung up on her.

Chrissie expected to feel remorse but didn't. She poured Froot Loops into a bowl and tried to decide what Rose would want her to do next. It didn't make sense to Chrissie that Anjelica was pursuing this.

She was pouring milk on her Froot Loops when it came to her that there must be something else in the diary. Not just Rose Lymond's secret.

A second secret.

A secret that would matter to Anjelica Lofft.

Chrissie closed her eyes and tried to remember every word she had read in that diary. But if there was a second secret, Chrissie could not come up with it. I should talk to Rose, thought Chrissie. But then I'd have to admit I read the diary. I'd have to admit I know the truth.

Putting a hand on the overpass railing, Rose simply vaulted over. It was the kind of thing she would never have done if she'd had time to think about it. What if she fell thirty feet to her death on the pavement below? What if she wasn't strong enough to vault over and got impaled against the railing? What if it would have been wiser to run forward or dash back?

But Rose didn't think, just leaped.

She was lucky. She was close to the start of the

bridge and her fall was only six or eight feet, cushioned by little bushes. Her roll downhill was punctuated by the stabs of sharp little cedars.

She somersaulted, feet hitting the hot pavement of the little country road. She staggered, got her balance, and ran under the bridge. It was damp in there, and dark. Water seeped through cracked concrete. She wasn't bleeding, thanks to the padded vest and her jeans, but she was good and bruised.

Had it been the SUV loitering at the top of the hill south of her? Rose knew her cars, because she was fifteen and thought constantly about what she would own if she could own one. And yet the vast number of cars had made her lose interest; they blurred until they were just traffic.

She berated herself for not identifying the vehicle. In memory she fought for detail, but she had caught none. She'd been busy saving her skin.

Above Rose, the car braked rather carefully, probably not even leaving a patch. It came to a stop in the emergency lane. Its bulky frame cast a shadow on the country road below.

Rose backed up into the depths of the tunnel, her heart pounding like tires on a warning strip. The shadow of the driver leaned over to see what had become of her. The sun was bright and the two shadows had the clarity of black paper cutouts.

Walk out and wave, she told herself. Let the poor soul know you weren't hit.

But she didn't move. Had the car wandered out of its

lane? Or left the lane deliberately? Had the driver felt like scaring any old orange-vested worker by the side of the road? Fair game, the way substitute teachers in school were usually considered fair game? Or, when her cap blew off, had the driver known Rose by her hair?

How deserted the little country road was. Above her, traffic raced by. Down here, it was quiet and empty. She yearned for a school bus or a delivery truck.

The driver shadow disappeared. In a moment, the car shadow also disappeared.

When her pulse eased off, she scrabbled back up her hill. No other car had stopped. Nobody had noticed anything. There was no one in the emergency lane and no dark SUV in sight.

Rose leaned on the top of her stick, staring at all the bad drivers of the world.

She didn't want to get on the bridge again. But if she didn't cross it, she wasn't going to reach the trash on that end of her half mile.

They're not grading me, she reminded herself. I'm not going to get C minus because I skip some of it.

She caught sight of the boy's baseball cap. It had been swept up the grassy slope she had just cleaned. Rose caught it and wept suddenly over the kindness of strangers.

When rehabilitation was over and Rose finally got home, her parents were sitting together, watching TV news. Rose hated television news. It made her queasy and uncertain, as if life, like tides, could come out from under her.

She stood silently, not wanting to let Mom and Dad know she was home. What would they say? So, darling, how was rehab? Do you have a future in trash? Are you going to be a good, talkative girl from now on?

The Loffts had had TVs in every single room, including Rose's own bath. In that huge, elegant house . . . so much furniture, so many windows, paintings, sculpture, tapestries, collections . . . commentators called back and forth like dinner guests, from room to room, from channel to channel.

Late that Friday night, alone in the guest room, sick of rereading her diary, Rose got out of bed to see who was there, but the conversation she'd been dimly hearing all night long came from televisions.

She went from room to room, bare feet noiseless on the thick carpets or shining hardwood, Oriental rugs or Mexican tiles. The house was not full of people. It was full of television images, quivering reflections of humanity.

Rose had crept back to her solitary room. Crawled between the sheets. Slept for hours, as if things might change while she was unconscious. But in the morning, things had not changed.

Nothing would change here, either, so Rose went into the TV room and squished herself between her parents. "I'm a trash expert now," she said.

Her mother sighed, stroking the thin blond hair and taking Rose's fingers in her own and examining them, as if she might find answers in the shape of Rose's nails.

Dad put his arm around her and gave her a fierce one-armed hug. He was a forgiving man. Except for one thing.

Nobody could forgive that.

CHAPTER EIGHT

In the morning, Rose found that she lacked the energy for school.

She lay in bed staring at the ceiling. Unlike Tabor, who could sleep and sleep, body molded into the mattress, sleep so deep he could hardly be shaken awake, Rose just woke up and got out of bed. She never lingered.

Not today.

I can't get up, she thought. School is too much. Ming and Chrissie and Alan and the police and Mom and Dad. They're all too much.

She decided to stay home with a sick headache. She had never suffered from such a malady, but Chrissie's mother quite routinely had migraines so bad she threw up. Rose had helped Mrs. Klein one horrible afternoon, bringing a hot-water bottle, lowering the shades, and mopping up the bathroom.

I can fake it, she said to herself. I'll tuck into a ball under the covers and whimper.

Her father was ready to stay home from work to nurse her. Or summon a grandparent to spend the day at her side. "Daddy, I'm going to sleep all day," Rose told him. "Don't fuss. Please?"

He was rumpled from sleep, having Tabor's tendency to stay in bed, but never allowing himself to do it. Rose loved him so much she could hardly bear it and hugged her pillow to keep from hugging him.

In a neutral voice that proclaimed she didn't believe a word of this sick headache stuff, Mom said, "I'll call every hour, Rose."

That would certainly keep Rose from going on any major expeditions.

Mom sat on the edge of Rose's bed. "Honey."

"My head is killing me," said Rose, closing her eyes.

"We've got a wide selection of medication," said her mother. "Aspirin, Tylenol, Sudafed, Motrin, the list goes on and on. I'm not arguing with your decision to stay home, honey. I just want you to know how much you are scaring me. And Daddy. Today is the assembly you've been so excited about. Who qualifies for summer abroad and how to apply. And you'd rather hide out under the covers?"

She had forgotten the assembly and the whole concept of summers abroad.

"Rose, tell me what is going on. Please."

Now a headache really did throb. Since when could you just sign up for headaches? "Mom, don't phone every hour. I need uninterrupted sleep."

Mom felt Rose's forehead and throat, ran her cool, slim fingers down Rose's arm to her wrist, and took her pulse. Then she kissed Rose's cheek, the way only Mom kissed, long and motionless, as if actually joining herself to Rose. "I'll call the school to let them know you're ill."

Rose, who never went back to sleep, whose capacity for sleep was precise and limited, had fallen asleep again before her parents even left the house. Her second sleep was deep, and she was way down inside it when the phone rang.

She woke with the thick, muddy mind of a nap, saw that it was eleven o'clock, and she had slept three hours. Three hours! At least her headache was gone. The phone rang again. Rose lurched around on the bed, throwing sheets and a blanket out of her way in a clumsy effort to get at the phone on the night table.

It would be Mom checking on her. She mumbled hello.

"Rose, this is Anjelica Lofft."

Rose was immobilized. She could feel a hundred things she hadn't felt a moment ago. The wrinkled bed-covers under her thighs. The damp sweat on her forehead. The cool plastic surface of the receiver.

She had not spoken to Anjelica in four years. During the whole week of school following Rose's visit to the lake estate, Anjelica had avoided her. When Rose handed Anjelica a thank-you note, Anjelica simply nodded and walked away. A few weeks later, Anjelica Lofft left public school and entered a private academy. The following year, she lived in England. The year after that, Rose had heard Anjelica was at boarding school.

Why would Anjelica Lofft make contact with Rose now?

It was a school day. How had she known Rose was home?

How had she known the female voice that answered was not Rose's mother or one of her many other relatives?

What did Anjelica Lofft want?

What do I want? thought Rose. She disconnected the phone gently, withdrawing her hand from the receiver as if it might have changed substance; become china or glass. She smoothed the blanket. Folded the hem of the top sheet neatly over it, adjusted corners and fluffed the pillow. In normal circumstances, Rose never made her bed. It was one of the few fights she constantly had with her mother. Oh, Mom, for heaven's sake, what do you think is going to happen to the bed? she would demand. The sheets are going to get dusty?

Rose pulled on her bathrobe and ran downstairs to check the locks on the doors.

They did not live in a town or a time when they worried about locking up. High crime in Rose's part of the world was shoplifting at the discount mall. The Lymonds and their neighbors rarely worried about personal safety. Dad locked the house at night, but during the day they left the doors open so relatives and friends could come and go. In the summer, they never bothered to close the doors, let alone lock them, and one of the sounds of Rose's childhood was the sound of wooden screens slapping against frames.

She locked herself in.

The phone rang again. Ring after ring trembled through the silent house, until finally the answering machine picked up. Rose, like the caller, listened to its little speech.

For years, Rose and Tabor alternated making the recordings. Tabor's month would feature rock music and screaming, while hers — even when she was only five or six — would be calm and careful. When Tabor turned sixteen, the whole thing embarrassed him and he refused to participate. Rose, aching for Tabor's approval, also refused, although she loved speaking into the recorder. Since then, Dad's voice had said pleasantly, *Hello. You've reached the Lymonds. Nobody is able to take your call. Please leave your name, the date, and your phone number and a short message, and somebody will get back to you. Thanks, and have a great day.*

"Dad," Tabor would tell him, "nobody needs all that. It's like you're putting an advice column on your answering machine. Loosen up."

How could it be that Rose and Dad were the ones who did not loosen up?

But it was not Anjelica trying a second time. It was Dad. "I hope I'm not waking you, sweetheart," he said into the machine. "You were asleep when Mom and I left for work and she felt awful that she'd been suspicious of your headache. She didn't want to wake you with phone calls after all. I said I'd check before lunchtime, so —"

Rose scooped up the kitchen phone. "Hi, Daddy, I'm here, I was just slow."

"Feeling better?"

"Lots. I slept till a minute ago. Isn't that amazing? I never go back to sleep. The headache's gone. I think I'm going to school after all and be there for my afternoon classes and then I have community service."

"It sounds so charitable when you call it community service," said her father. "As if you're reading out loud to lonely patients in nursing homes."

"Okay, then I have pseudojail time," said Rose.

Her father sighed. "I'll let your mother know you're headed back to school."

"Thanks, Daddy. Don't worry about me."

He assured her that he would always worry about her; that's what fathers did when their daughters were being idiots.

Under the circumstances, Rose could hardly argue with his description of her. She went upstairs to put the yellow bathrobe back on its hook. She had so rarely worn the robe that it still had creases from its original purchase. She took the key she had not touched in years, inserted it in the headboard keyhole, and opened her cubby.

It was empty, of course.

Her only secret was gone.

She dressed to look good in school and also to be properly protected against trash and dust. Downstairs, she got a glass of orange juice and drank it slowly.

Outside the sky was crayon blue, furrowed and whipped with soft white clouds.

Just so had the sky been crayon blue on the Friday she skipped swimming and came home early. On her way back to the Y to go to swim class after all, Rose had picked up fallen weeping willow wands and peeled away the soft bark. She liked to pretend she was an Indian woman and had baskets to weave. She remembered slicing them through the air, listening to the sharp, cruel whistle they made, as if she were whipping a bare back.

By the time the phone rang, Rose had forgotten she was screening calls. "Hello?"

"It's Anjelica. Don't hang up."

"You're here!" shrieked Ming when Rose opened the classroom door to slip in late. "We thought the police had probably locked you up permanently."

"Or Milton Lofft tied you up in his cellar," suggested Richard.

"Or Milton Lofft gave you so much money that you left the country to live on a sunny Mediterranean isle," said Halsey.

"Or I woke up this morning with a sick headache," said Rose, "so I went back to sleep for a while. You are all future screenwriters. Mrs. Baker," she said to her English teacher, "I apologize for the disruption."

"It isn't a disruption at all," said Mrs. Baker, giggling as if she were twelve instead of forty. "It's perfect timing, Rose. Guess what. You're going to hate me," she said happily. "For our free-style writing today, I assigned two paragraphs on Why Rose Lymond Stole a Police Car." Mrs. Baker's big happy smile continued to decorate her face.

You're right, thought Rose. I hate you. You are a rodent. I'm going to charge you with harassment.

The hair on twenty-five heads gleamed in the light. Twenty-five faces turned her way. "I thank each of you for your kindness at a difficult time and especially for the example set by our teacher," said Rose softly.

Half the class was shamed. Heads dropped and faces flushed.

The other half was delighted. She was a good talk show guest, the sort who filmed well. They grinned and hoped for more.

Rose tried to stare Mrs. Baker into an apology. But the woman was giggling with the wrong half of the class, scurrying around collecting the Why Did Rose, etc., papers. "Chrissie, your paper is blank," cried Mrs. Baker.

"I had nothing to say on the topic," said Chrissie politely. "Give me an F, please."

Over the heads of their classmates and the white rectangles of waving paper, past the thick body of Mrs. Baker in the dress she had outgrown years ago, Chrissie Klein and Rose Lymond looked at each other.

She knows, thought Rose.

Sick shock enveloped Rose. It had never occurred to her that one of her many girlfriends spending the night might have read the diary. Why had she not protected herself against such a thing? How many stupid things could she do all in a row, anyway?

But that's when slumber parties ended, she thought. We outgrew overnights in seventh grade. My very last slumber party ever was the weekend after I went to the Loffts'. I didn't protect myself because I didn't have more overnights. Which means Chrissie read my diary right then and there. She's known all this time. Why didn't I think of that? I just didn't. I knew Mom and Dad would never trespass on me. Tabor wouldn't bother, he didn't care what I thought out loud or on paper. And if any of them *had* read the diary, we wouldn't be in the police car mess. We'd be in another mess altogether.

Rose felt like dust, suspended in the sun shaft. She sat at her usual desk, from which she did not have a sight line toward Chrissie. She liked to sit in front because she liked to follow the teacher's remarks and never miss anything on the blackboard. Perhaps it was time for a change in attitude and seating position.

When class ended, she found herself in the hall with Chrissie. "Thank you for standing up for me," Rose told her. She was glad Chrissie was so much taller. She could look at Chrissie's chin instead of into her eyes.

"Sure. But that's not the thing, Rose," said Chrissie very softly. "The thing is that people aren't going to understand."

Rose shrugged. It was the first real shrug of her life. "I don't care."

"You've got to care, Rose." Chrissie breathed intensely. "There's something else going on. Anjelica called me yesterday."

Rose looked up, confused. A little frightened. "Anjelica called *you?*"

"Exactly. I —" Chrissie broke off. "Oh, hi, Ming. How are you?"

"Super, thanks. Rose, I hope you weren't upset by class. We were just having fun."

"I was upset," said Rose, thinking — Anjelica called Chrissie? But — "And it wasn't fun, Ming."

"Oh, lighten up!" snapped Ming. "You're the one who stole the cop car. You have to expect results from that kind of thing."

Rose was descended from a person who didn't think about results. Had she inherited that trait?

I'm going to throw up, she thought. I didn't fake the sick headache after all. "Chrissie," she said desperately, "I have one of those headaches like your mother gets. I'm going to be sick."

"Girls' room," said Chrissie instantly. "Run. Don't mess up the hall, it's just another confrontation nobody needs." She grabbed Rose's arm and they hauled around the corner and made it with no time to spare. Rose retched horribly into the nearest toilet.

Ming came, too, soaking a paper towel in cold water so Rose could wash her face.

Go away, thought Rose.

But Ming didn't go away. The subject that was so vital remained untouchable.

"I have practice after school," said Chrissie uncertainly. She was taller than Rose by five inches and taller than Ming by eight. It gave her control over the situation, and yet her voice did not sound as if she knew what was happening.

And why did Rose herself feel that she, too, did not know what was happening? It was her diary, for heaven's sake. She was the one person who surely knew exactly what was happening. "And I have community service," she said firmly. "Or whatever you want to call it. Fresh air jail."

The girls stood in the stinking bathroom and laughed helpessly. "Oh, Rose," said Chrissie. "It's so impossible. It's so not you! Or it *is* you, and I never knew you. And the way you handled Mrs. Baker! Awesome."

"Half the class didn't get it," said Rose.

Chrissie explained rudely where that half of the class could go and the girls laughed again, even though Ming had been in the wrong half.

And because friends were worth so much, Rose forgave Ming for being a rodent.

And because friends were worth so much, Chrissie decided not to force the Anjelica issue right now. Time enough later.

CHAPTER NINE

R ose enjoyed trash.

The sky was intensely blue, the air sharp and tasty. The wind never stopped and the trash whirled away before she could stab it, playing tag with her, hiding out in the trees. She stayed on the safe side of the guardrail.

She did not think of profound things or shallow. She did not think of friend, family, or foe. She did not think of present or past.

She did not think.

Dinner that evening was almost pleasant. Mom was glad Rose had gone to school after all and Dad hoped she would not get more headaches. Mom wanted to know if Rose planned to apply for the summer abroad program. Dad said anxiously that he would miss Rose a lot while Mom said Rose needed to spread her wings.

Rose said nothing, but they were getting used to it now and let it pass, and she went up to her room thinking that she would do homework, because homework was what she always did on school nights, but she couldn't get started.

She felt odd and floaty. Over and over she heard the

voice on the phone saying, "Rose. This is Angelica Lofft."

She listened to herself hanging up once.

Listened to herself hanging up a second time, having exchanged not one syllable with that ghost of the past.

About eight-thirty, her father tapped on the door. "Rose," he said, anxious enough for any ten people, "the police are here again."

Rose's heartbeat doubled. She did not have the strength for this. How did people become career criminals? Why didn't they drop dead at an early age from the stress? "Honestly, Dad," she said, trying to sound like an ordinary grumbling teenager. "When they come to the door," she added, opening her own, "you don't have to invite them in for milk and cookies. Send them home."

"They're my only source of information right now about my own daughter," he said.

Rose trembled at this misstatement. "Well, let's go downstairs and see what they're here for this time."

"I don't want you to say anything until Mr. Travis is here."

"That was my plan, too, except I'm not going to say anything *after* Mr. Travis comes, either, because there isn't anything to say."

"Maybe not, honey, but the police said this is urgent, so we're waiting for your lawyer. Rose, I'm frightened for you. I'm frightened for all of us. Please take this seriously. I cannot fathom why you do not trust me."

"I trust you," she whispered. But of course she did not. Of every terrible thing that had come from that weekend, this was the most terrible. She wept on his shoulder — two short beats of sob — and then pulled together. "Sorry, Daddy. I guess it's wearing me down."

"It's wearing me down, too, Rose!"

She shrugged — at her father, whom she loved more than anybody! — and walked out, saying nothing more.

On the stairs, he paused and seemed to reach a decision. "Rose, I know you have enough to worry about, but I have a new worry and I'm going to tell you what it is. This is expensive. Travis bills us for every hour. Every quarter hour, actually. I accept that you're not going to trust me. So please trust him. What you tell him will be confidential, even from me. Even from your mother."

She had not known silence would cost anything. Not in dollars, anyway. Her parents were struggling, what with Tabor in such an expensive college and their share of paying for Nannie's aides. "I'm sorry," she said helplessly. "Maybe I could pay you back. When I'm sixteen I can get a job. That's what I'll do. It'll be a debt for me to repay."

Rose felt better. Time would pass. She would turn sixteen; she could square herself with her parents. She smiled a real smile at her father, but he looked as if he could toss her down the stairs because of that smile. "I don't know where this is going, Rose," said her father. "You seem very sure of yourself. I'm not sure. Milton Lofft is described in financial journals as a cutthroat competitor. It's one thing to cut somebody's throat metaphorically, in order to get a better product and larger profits. But Frannie Bailey had her throat cut in real life. And you're standing in the middle of that."

She gasped. "Her throat was cut? But —"

He shook his head. "I'm just using the phrase. I'm desperate to get your attention, Rose. As I recall, she was hit over the head with something. Maybe you're hoping to be hit over the head with something. But I'm *not* hoping for that. I want this over and I want my daughter back."

She had no choice but to shrug again.

In her living room — hers! — two police in uniform leaned against the mantel. A woman in a silk blouse and challis skirt held a clipboard and a phone. And a man in a charcoal-gray suit, like an ad in a glossy magazine, stood by the bay window with Rose's mother. Rose was shocked to see her mother crying.

She felt a surge of panic. What could this be about? She wondered, horrified, sick, if something had happened to Anjelica.

Had Anjelica called upon Rose for help? Only to be refused twice in five minutes?

Rose's head whirled. She of all people ought to grasp what was going on. But she didn't. It was as if she had designed and cut a jigsaw puzzle and now she herself could not put it together.

"Rose," said the man in the suit, "my name is CJ Pierson."

Rose wanted to tell him that boys stopped calling themselves CJ by seventh grade. After that, even if their names were really Clarence Jenks, they used their names. "How do you do, Mr. Pierson."

"I'm a detective, Rose. Your situation has bumped up a notch."

Rose said nothing. She focused on his tie. She loved men's ties, the sheen of the silk, the shaping of the knot. She loved buying ties for her father, who did not love wearing them, and now had a large collection of completely untouched neckties. Perhaps by the time Rose became an impressive figure in science or history, women would be wearing ties and she would have a big start on everybody else.

"One of the men picking up trash with you yesterday," said CJ Pierson, "reported that a dark green Chevy Tahoe intentionally tried to hit the worker standing on Willow Creek Road Bridge."

I didn't make it up, thought Rose, relieved. I wasn't a jerk when I leaped over the railing and tumbled down onto the pavement below. I didn't know it was Willow Creek Road. Now I know.

She was aware of how much she loved facts. She would hold onto that new fact — the name of the road — and it would strengthen her against another fact — that somebody had tried to run her down. Although she didn't remember the vehicle either being green or being a Tahoe.

"There was also a report from a driver calling it in

on his car phone; he said it was a black Durango intentionally trying to hit somebody on a trash detail. Both sources thought the highway worker was a man. But it was you, wasn't it?"

What if I hadn't jumped? she thought.

She imagined relatives gathering for her funeral, rafts of them filling the pews, weeping and crying, *Why? Why darling, sweet Rose?*

She said to CJ Pierson, "Huh?"

Her father grabbed her. He was trembling, his hands rough in his fear. "Rose, what is going on?" He shook her, trying to find the daughter who had vanished on him. "Rose! How can you stand there so blandly? How can you just say '*huh?*' as if you don't have enough brains to come in out of the rain? I can't understand a thing that's going on! You have been the perfect daughter! And now —"

"Daddy, calm down. Nothing like that happened. It must have been somebody else. Both witnesses said it was a man that the SUV nearly hit. Besides, although a Durango and a Tahoe are both midsized, they don't look that much alike, and green isn't the same as black, so those don't sound like very solid witnesses to me."

Her father stepped away from her. He reached for Mom, who was sobbing audibly now. "Oh, Tommy," she cried. Rose loved it when her mother called him Tommy instead of Thomas. It made Dad sound young and Mom in love.

CJ Pierson seemed to find Rose more interesting

than he had a moment ago. His voice was neither angry nor demanding, just working to follow her thoughts. "Rose, why deny it?"

I do deny it, she thought. Nobody would try to run me over. Or if they did, it doesn't have anything to do with this. It was just a road rage nutcase and I happened to be there, a nice bright orange anonymous target.

"Everything you've done defies rational explanation, Rose. Yet from what I hear, you are a very rational young woman."

Rose tried to look dense instead.

"Who owns a green or a black SUV?" her mother demanded of the police. She was shouting in her fear. She had not wiped the tears from her cheeks. She looked awful. "Does Milton Lofft?"

"Yes, he has two, as a matter of fact," said the detective. "A black Benz and a green Range Rover. Problem is, half the population owns a dark SUV, Mrs. Lymond. Your son's friend Alan Finney has a black Explorer. I have a steel gray Xterra, and my brother-in-law has a dark green Grand Cherokee. Eleven teachers in your daughter's school drive dark SUVs. I bet I saw another half dozen parked in driveways on this street. Just for starters. So, Rose. You got any more detail on that car? You gonna be able to tell us the make? Model? Year? Plate numbers? You recognize the driver?"

Rose had forgotten that Alan Finney drove a black Explorer. Alan . . . who had asked which highway she would be working on. Her mind thrashed around like a fish on the sand. She stuck to her original lines because she had no others. "I didn't see anything, Detective Pierson," she said. It felt awkward to address him like that. "I don't know anything and why you won't believe me, I cannot imagine."

"Rose! We're not dealing with the weekend you visited the Loffts!" shouted her father. "We're dealing with somebody trying to run over you. Thousands of pounds of metal. Why didn't you tell us? What's the matter with you, Rose? You have to stop this nonsense! Somebody wants to hurt you!" He let go of Mom, who was still crying, and he said brokenly, "Rose, what would our lives be without you? There simply cannot be a good enough reason for your silence."

She had never dreamed how deeply this invasion would stab. How badly silence would work as a strategy. But she didn't have another one.

"They're going to talk to everybody now," said her mother, wiping away tears. "Your English teachers, in case you ever wrote a revealing essay. Your softball coach, in case you ever confided in her. Your art teacher. What kind of person will you look like when they're done? It will look as if you're some —"

Her father sprang immediately to her defense. "Now, Julia. Rose will look fine, because she is."

"Fine but stupid," said CJ Pierson. "Rose, a woman was murdered. Can you understand that? A hard, tough, demanding, high-energy woman who had the world on a string. Somebody ended her life very simply. One heavy rock against one fragile skull. Maybe she was as stupid as you at the end, maybe not. We don't know much about Frannie Bailey's death. Whoever you're protecting, Rose, whether it's Milton Lofft or somebody else, that person has decided he or she cannot count on your silence. That person has decided that eventually, you'll tell us what you saw. So it's better if you're dead."

Oh, no. It was infinitely better to be alive. Rose loved her life. The whole problem was that her life was precious just as it existed. She could allow nothing to interfere.

Being murdered would indeed interfere with life as Rose knew it.

"So what's next, Rose?" said CJ Pierson, his voice getting louder. "We gonna find out we don't know much about your death, either?"

Rose's mother put her hands over her ears, wincing at the word "death."

"You hoping for a future, Rose? College? Career? Wedding? Babies? A home of your own? Whaddaya want out there, Rose?" CJ Pierson stepped into her stare spot.

Rose's hands were so cold she wanted mittens.

"Rose," said her mother very softly. "Are we on your list of reasons to stay alive?"

Rose saw her parents very clearly at that moment: her father in such bad shape that even a relative stranger like Augusta was upset by it; her mother cut to the bone by Rose's sudden change of personality; both of them in terror for their little girl's life and safety.

She knew then that she was going to have to tell.

How would she do it? In what order? Which people would she include? With what words would she explain?

And when she was done — what would their world be?

Which kind of shattered world was better — one with silence or one with explanation?

She held out her arms to her parents, who sprang forward, as if thinking that explanations and long paragraphs would come along with hugs. Her cheek pressed against Dad's shirt, and she saw that one of the buttons had come off at some point and been stitched back on. The thread did not quite match. Rose imagined her mother standing over the ironing board, threading the needle.

CJ Pierson sighed. "Okay, Rose. We aren't going to waste more time. You got second thoughts, you call us. You're not gonna do traffic detail again. How about we assign you clerical work in the police department? You willing to do that?"

"Awesome," said Rose, before she could stop herself.

Everybody laughed for a moment, even Rose, and then the strangers drove away, and Rose was left with the parents to whom she was now a stranger.

They're suffering too much, she thought. Tell them. . . . But once they know, they'll suffer even more. So don't tell them.

Her parents had coffee. Mom could not pour without spilling. Finally she gave up. "Rose, do you know I can't sleep? I get up every few hours all night long and look in on you. I haven't done that since you were a newborn. I used to be afraid of crib death. I worried all the time when you and Tabor were babies. I used to tremble that we'd put you safely to sleep one night and in the morning you'd be blue and silent and dead. I was so glad when you got beyond the age for crib death. I thought I'd never be so scared for your life as I was the first few months. But I was wrong. I'm that scared now."

Rose could not look at her mother. She looked instead at one of the family portraits on the wall, a beautiful photograph of her parents before they had had children. Her father — so young! So slim and so much hair. Her mother — slender as a high school girl, with hair and makeup on which she clearly spent hours. Now they were both chunky, Dad's hair merely a fringe. There was hardly a trace in him of the eager, exuberant young man with the lovely young wife.

Tell, thought Rose, tell them now and get it over with.

But she had used silence one time too many.

Her mother slammed the coffeepot down, and since it was glass, it smashed on the table and hot coffee flooded the place mats and dripped on the floor. "You explain to me what's going on, young lady!" shouted her mother. "Don't you dare pull any fast ones with me."

You pulled a fast one once, thought Rose, and for the first time, Rose slightly hated her mother. The only surprising thing was that it had taken so long.

The hate was satisfying and exonerating. Inside the

hate, Rose could be silent forever. "I'll clean up the coffee," she said primly.

The hate had vanished before she reached the paper towels, but her parents had vanished before she got back with them. She heard doors slamming as they chose solitude over another minute in their daughter's presence.

She wondered why Anjelica Lofft had called twice. Whether she would call again.

And whether it had been a black Explorer that had waited so patiently in the emergency lane to see who wore the orange trash vest.

CHAPTER TEN

Saturday afternoon, from two to five, Rose Lymond found herself at the police department, assigned to CJ Pierson. She knew from two days of transport van gossip that nobody got rehabilitated on a weekend. Saturday and Sunday were your own, in which presumably you tried to consolidate your gains, thinking about your crimes, planning to omit future ones. On Monday, you arrived in good spirits for more rehabilitation, eager to improve.

Her parents and the police must have decided on a Saturday schedule for Rose. If only Rose were as tall and strong as Megan Moran. Then she could look down on people. CJ Pierson could not be so relentlessly in charge if Rose were taller. Chrissie, at five ten, truly mourned her lack of height, and for the first time, Rose understood.

"Hello, Rose," he said cheerfully.

She decided to be cheerful right back. It was a weapon she had not yet used. "Hello, Detective Pierson," she said brightly. "What fun. Look at all the stray papers on your desk. I hope I get to file. Don't worry if I throw a lot out. I've developed a trash habit." This sort of flippant banter was so unlike Rose that it undid her instead of him; she felt her chin tremble and her eyes water.

"You know, Rose, you're growing on me," he said. "The problem I see, though, is what's gonna be growing on your grave if you don't talk."

Rose pulled herself together. "A person's community service time is not the time in which a person should be interrogated by a law officer. A person being rehabilitated should work diligently and not be distracted. Concentration —"

"Yeah, have a seat, Rose. I'm looking through some old newspapers. I thought you might want to browse with me."

Rose sat before she saw the dates of the newspapers. She was very sorry she had sat down. She picked out a spot on the window to stare at. The windows were filthy and there were a multitude of spots to stare at, some of them alive and moving. Perhaps she would assign herself Windex and paper towels.

"Friday through Wednesday," said CJ Pierson. "Of a famous weekend. Come on, Rose. Rehabilitate yourself. Read every word and tell me what you think."

His shirt was white, with heavy starch. The collar was very crisp above his fine tie, a silky horsetail gray flecked with tiny dark red diamonds. Rose distracted herself by listing the people she felt like strangling with that tie.

CJ Pierson spread a four-year-old Friday paper on

his desk and began tapping headlines and advertisements, announcements and fillers. His pencil eraser made a soft, friendly little thud on the newsprint.

Rose had never glanced at the newspapers back then. She had been twelve, after all. How many twelve-year-olds curled up with a newspaper? She didn't know what was in the papers. But since the news of Frannie Bailey's murder had not been available to television until Monday, it wouldn't have been in the newspaper, either.

"So here's my current guess," said CJ Pierson, smiling at her. He had a nice smile. It reminded her of Grandfather's, whose portraits were everywhere in Nannie's house and with whom Nannie was convinced she would live again after death. Grandfather had not been a talker, like Nannie and Dad and Tabor. He had been an audience.

They all want to be my audience, she thought. They all want to sit quietly while I entertain them with my story.

"See, what I've been thinking is," said the detective, "suppose we're heading in the wrong direction when we question you about Frannie Bailey. Suppose the real story is here in these newspapers."

Another sick headache began with a faint pounding like a train in the distance, and the absolute knowledge that the train would arrive and explode inside her head. How awful to go through this routinely, like Chrissie's mother.

"There was a hit-and-run the same night Milton

Lofft was driving you to the lake estate," said CJ Pierson in a slow, informative voice. "Did you see that hit-and-run, Rose? It was never solved. Was the driver somebody you care about? Was it your brother, Tabor? Was it his friend Alan? Guy you've had a crush on for years? Or was it somebody else in his band? Verne maybe? Who quit the band that weekend? And never drove again?"

Rose could not prevent a shudder, but she did not look up to see if the detective had registered it. Of course he had. That's what police did, they read body language.

In the gentlest voice, so similar to her great-grandfather's that Rose almost caved in, CJ Pierson said, "Rose, there was a fatality. A man was killed in that hit-and-run. He had no children, but he left a wife with multiple sclerosis who was completely dependent on him for nursing care. With him dead, she had to be put in an institution. She's not doing well, Rose. She still cries for her dead husband."

Rose put a hand over her mouth. Four years and some poor hospitalized woman who couldn't walk by herself was still sobbing for the man who had loved her. It was a horrible story. She could not think about it.

With large red-handled utility scissors, CJ Pierson cut out the article on the hit-and-run. He taped it to a piece of blank white paper and outlined it in thick black marker. Then he photocopied it and handed Rose the copy. "For reference."

The article looked like a jail. Black-edged and barred.

"Read it, please, Rose."

She read it. Her suffering did not compare with what this poor woman was enduring. In fact, Rose wasn't suffering if you compared her to the widow in the hospital.

"Are you protecting the driver who killed her husband?" the detective asked. He wasn't being combative. He was being nice. She pictured him visiting the widow in the hospital, being nice to her, too.

It took two tries but Rose finally found her voice. "I'm not protecting anybody. Really and truly. I didn't see anything. I don't know anything. Really and truly." She was starting to cry. She pressed her fingertips hard against her temples and eyes to beat down the tears.

"Your brother got into lots of trouble when he was in high school, Rose. Stupid, minor trouble. Stuff nobody cares about anymore. Tabor didn't have his driver's license back then, of course. He was a few months short of sixteen back then. But that doesn't mean he didn't drive, does it, Rose?"

Rose folded the photocopy neatly in half and drew her thumbnail down the crease. Then she folded it in half again.

"Lot of six-packs in that car?" asked CJ Pierson. "Lot of teenage boys having a lot of beer? Is that it? You protecting the whole band?"

"Please believe me," whispered Rose.

"I can't believe you, Rose. You didn't steal a police car because of nothing. You stole a police car because of something."

Rose had no tissues. She wiped her eyes on her sleeve.

"Is your secret worth dying for?" he asked.

Detective Pierson drove her home.

He didn't pull in the driveway but stopped in the road to let her out. He said, "Rose, you call me if you have second thoughts, okay?"

Second thoughts! Rose was on her ten thousandth thought. "Thank you for the ride," she said dully. "I'll see you next week." She looked up at her house, which again tonight was not going to be a sanctuary from trouble. Yellow light spilled from the kitchen windows on the darkening grass. Very clearly she saw into the kitchen, saw who was getting a glass from the cupboard next to the sink.

Tabor.

Rose faced the police car, although she was not large enough to block the view. She stood very still, as if Detective Pierson were her child and she must watch and guide his safety as he headed down the street. He shook his head, frustrated by her, and finally drove away, without, she hoped, seeing who was here.

Tabor home for the weekend?

But he'd be back for the summer in only a few weeks anyway. The airline ticket must have been so expensive.

Mom and Dad must be hoping Tabor would make her talk.

He wouldn't have the remotest idea how to do that, since Tabor's entire life was built upon being the one doing the talking. Tabor loved the sound of his own voice. If Tabor could not be the center of things, he didn't come.

The household had pivoted around Tabor, and then, he was gone. College absorbed him as paper towels absorb a spill. He left no trace.

Tabor had chosen a college as far away from family as he could get. Dad had been crushed, having always thought that family was the finest gift he presented his children. To which Tabor basically said, "Yup, and I'm out of here."

Rose had to face him this evening, and tomorrow probably through church and Sunday dinner, and probably he'd take a midafternoon flight back to college. It was a long time to hold off a brother.

Her strategy would be exuberance. She would go in like a cheerleader, make him the center of things, which he loved; get him to talk, which he loved.

Go to bed early, which Rose was going to love.

"Tabor!" she yelled, running up the driveway. "What are you doing home? Tabor! I'm so glad to see you!"

The family poured out of the house.

Even in the short time since February break, when he was last home, Tabor had changed. Twenty was just so much older than nineteen. He reminded her of Dad in the photo, eager and exuberant and ready to take on the world.

How glad Dad was to see Tabor. How bright and joyful it made the father to be near the son. Rose watched her father circling his son, making little offerings of conversation and compliments, stories and jokes. Dad was thrilled.

It strengthened Rose. She had lied to CJ Pierson, of course. There were people to protect.

"How was rehabilitation?" asked Tabor.

"I've become a good person at last," said Rose. "Filing at the police department is very character building."

"What kind of stuff did you file?"

"Patrolmen's notes on crimes," she said. "DNA results. Placement services for retired police dogs."

"You're such a liar," said Tabor. "I bet you washed windows."

"I tried. *They* certainly don't wash windows. I'm starving to death, Mom. What are we having for dinner? Or are we going out to celebrate Tabor being home?" On the one hand, Rose was way too tired for dining out. A bowl of cornflakes was all she could face. On the other hand, they couldn't interrogate her in public.

"I've been cooking since Dad left to pick Tabor up at the airport," said Mom. "We're having a Louisiana shrimp, chicken, okra, and rice dish I learned how to make on the Food Channel."

Tabor and Rose moaned in unison. "At least skip the okra," said Tabor. "It's the slimiest vegetable."

"I want my children to be sophisticated diners," said Mom.

"Since when is okra sophisticated?" asked Tabor. "Anyway, you lose on the sophisticated diner front. I live on pizza. I never touch a vegetable except tomato sauce."

"Fine," said their mother. "Pick out the okra and move it to the side of your plate. Now, while I finish fixing the salad, you two sit out here on the porch and catch up."

"Is this how we refer to the little episode of snatching a cop car?" asked Tabor.

"Perhaps a subject of greater interest," said Rose, "would be my phragmites research."

"Nobody cares about your phragmites inoculant," said Tabor. "Or does it work now? In which case, I want a percent of the profit."

Rose admitted that it did not work. Tabor did not care about a percent of nothing.

Their parents went inside, shutting the door firmly to imply that secrets could now be exchanged in the safety of the outdoors.

Tabor sat on the porch steps, resting his chin on his knees. He patted the step next to him and she sat. Shadows poured into their laps. The soft air smelled of narcissus.

"Bus to the airport, one hour," said Tabor, lifting his fingers and ticking them off. "Wait for plane, one hour. First flight, two hours. Change planes and layover, one hour. Second flight, three hours. Drive back home, one hour. I have spent a nine-hour day, Rose, dwelling on your crimes."

Yeah, well, I've spent four years, she thought. "Congratulations," she said mildly. "That's probably more time than you've considered your sister in your whole life."

"You bet," said Tabor. "I spent my nine hours denying that my steady, sober little sister changed so much that she's off stealing cop cars for a hobby. Denying that my little sister has enemies. Denying that people out there want to mow her down so she won't talk. Denying that she has anything to talk about."

"You may continue to deny all of that," said Rose in her most comforting voice. "I stole one police car. It is not developing into a hobby. I have no enemies. Nobody is mowing me down."

Tabor nodded for a while. "Rosie, I never read your diary. I never trespassed on you. I never sneaked into your room and stole the key and opened up your diary. Do I get points?"

"No. The reason you didn't read my diary isn't because you're saintly. It's because you knew it wouldn't be interesting."

"I was wrong, huh?"

"Tabor, convince Mom and Dad there's nothing to worry about."

"Yeah," said Tabor. "Like telling people who live under an exploding volcano not to worry; it's only lava."

They laughed.

"Alan says you're just shrugging about the whole thing," said Tabor. "Rose, from the way Mom and Dad tell it, there's nothing to shrug about. Aside from the fact that you've now got a juvenile record —"

"You're just jealous."

"I'm totally jealous. I was always proud of the way you and I divided up the burden of being kids. I made trouble, you were perfect. It was a good fit."

They laughed.

"So you ordered Alan to be friends with me," said Rose. "Why was that?"

"I ordered him to give me a second opinion of what's going on. Mom and Dad are ballistic and you won't come to the phone. What are you going to give me now — the Aunt Sheila treatment?"

Rose stared at him.

"Come on," said Tabor impatiently. "You haven't talked to Aunt Sheila in years. You won't even write her thank-you notes if she remembers presents. Last time even *I* was embarrassed and I thanked her for your Christmas present in *my* letter."

How strange and terrible was memory. It cascaded down in a waterfall of its own. Drops of thought, rainbows of understanding, splashes of depth.

The memory of Aunt Sheila and Mom talking blended with the memory of Mr. Lofft's book tape and Anjelica's movie tape and the police then and the police now asking the same questions. Rose might have been sitting on the leather reclining seat in the big brown Navigator, listening to Anjelica open the bag of chips, looking out the window, and seeing nothing but the interior of her soul.

"Let's help Mom set the table," she said, getting up before Tabor could stop her. She stepped inside and tripped over his luggage just behind the door. Tabor traveled with more possessions than a Victorian explorer.

Rose had taken Tabor's duffel bag that weekend to go to Anjelica's. Aunt Sheila had been genuinely annoyed. "Oh, don't take that tatty old thing. It stinks of sweaty sneakers. Here. Use my suitcase. See how pretty it is, with flowers on the fabric?" Rose had refused the loan of the suitcase.

"That smells wonderful, Mom," said Rose, entering the kitchen. "What's the spice?" She didn't listen to the answer. She was busy avoiding her father's look. He knew perfectly well she didn't care what the spice was.

Dinner was delightful. Rose even tried the okra. It was as squishy and tasteless as she remembered. The shrimp, chicken, and rice, however, were creamy and thick and wonderful.

Tabor talked about himself, and in Lymond fashion had wonderful stories about college and friends and class, failure and success.

All Lymonds talked. Their specialty was family stories. Lymond ancestors ran away from home, worked in a coal mine, fished for cod, died at sea, and specialized in losing lots of money. When Rose was little, though, she loved her mother's stories best, because Mom's stories were always about Rose. Mom used to take out one of the old calendars she saved each year, flip to any page, and start talking. "Look, Rosie!" she'd say. "When you were five, you had a December ballet program.

Look at this little note. I was responsible for bringing food to the reception."

"Tell me what I did," Rose would demand.

"You were a snowflake. You snowed so beautifully. I was so proud. All your grandparents and greats were there. Let's find the right album and look at your snow photographs."

O, family, thought Rose. I cannot be the one to damage the beauty of our family.

She held herself far away from the knowledge of who had really damaged the beauty of the family.

Mom set out an ice cream cake, Tabor's favorite dessert but not Rose's. Then Mom sliced through the frozen cake, saying in the cheery voice of one giving a toddler extra long tub time with a new yellow ducky, "You know what let's do now? Let's reconstruct that weekend."

Rose left the table. "I'll be washing my hair."

"You're staying here," said her mother sharply.

"I've told you a hundred times, I have nothing to say."

"Stay here, Rose," said her father. "We have to work this through. Your mother and Tabor and I are part of this nightmare whether we want to be or not."

You're *not* part of it, thought Rose. Whether you want to be or not.

She flung herself into the one chair in which she could not be touched but would be fully protected by the wide, curving wings of the upholstered arms. She pretended the protruding arms were the veiled sides of her nun's habit and part of her silence.

Mom marched to the shelf in the TV room where she kept the used-up engagement calendars and the photograph albums. Most people had gone years ago to complex date books of the Filofax type or handheld computers. But the Lymond family engagement calendar still sat on the counter in the kitchen below the wall phone, next to a mug of pencils and Post-its in many colors. Written in Mom's tiny neat hand on those calendars were the details of their lives: dentist appointments, car pool responsibilities, committee meetings, ball games. Rose knew now that there had been omissions in those entries.

"Here we go," said Mom, finding November just where it always was, toward the end. "Sheila was here that weekend."

"Aunt Sheila was here two weeks," said Tabor. "I remember because I was pretty sick of her by the time that visit ended. Rose was the lucky one, getting away for a few days."

Nobody corrected this slight on Aunt Sheila.

"We did a lot with Sheila that week," said Mom, sounding pleased. "The new aquarium, the theater, the car races. On Friday, Rose had swim class after school, Mr. Lofft was due to get Rose at four-thirty, Tabor's band was here to practice, and then you and I took Sheila into the city, Thomas, to see a play."

Rose maneuvered herself upside down in the armchair so that her spine lay on the seat, her legs in their faded jeans stuck up the back, and her head hung toward the floor.

"You used to do that when you were little," said her father affectionately. He could never hold onto his anger. "You were taking gymnastics and wanted to be famous on a balance beam. You were always twisting yourself into pretzels so you'd become flexible."

"I don't remember that," said Tabor. "How come you didn't stick with gymnastics, Rose?"

"I wasn't flexible. Or good. I just wanted to wake up one morning and be famous."

"If Milton Lofft comes to trial, you'll get your wish," said Tabor.

Rose tucked herself into a doughnut.

"Now, Saturday you had a football game, Tabor, and we sat with the Finneys."

"We won, too," said Tabor. Tabor never forgot his victories. Actually, he never forgot his defeats, either. Tabor was fond of thinking about his past activities.

"Saturday night your band played someplace called The Train Whistle."

"Juice bar," said Tabor. "It flourished for about two weekends. The thing about Saturday was Verne calls me up just before I leave for the football game to say he's quitting because he has better things to do." Tabor still sounded offended. "I think it's a real testimony to my sportsmanship that I could still play a winning game and go straight from the locker room to arrange rides and a substitute bass player."

Rose waited for them to ask about Milton Lofft and it took, by her watch, twelve more seconds.

"Tell me one thing about Milton Lofft's," said Tabor. "Did he really have a sixteen-car garage?"

"Yes."

"And?"

"And it faced front and back, eight cars to a side, each one in its separate little garage."

"What did you get to drive?"

"I didn't."

"You are being so annoying," said Tabor. "This can't have anything to do with anything. You can at least describe the cars."

"No, I can't, because we didn't drive after all, even though Anjelica said we would. It was just some empty boast of hers."

"What did you do?"

All the Loffts really did was watch television. Like so many driven people, Mr. Lofft had to be up to speed on every event in the world, the nation, the state, and the region. The house thrummed with the voices of reporters.

"We just ran from one activity to another," said Rose, upside down. "We were busy, you know, the way little kids are."

This was largely untrue. They had been seventh graders. Rose had left behind her little-kid behavior, and Anjelica perhaps never possessed it. She and Anjelica just walked around in an odd, slow silence, as if Anjelica were wishing she had invited somebody else.

"Did Milton Lofft mention the murder?" asked Tabor. "What was he wearing? Was it bloodstained?"

Rose felt a sudden surge of wrath toward her brother. All her life, he had assigned her to fetch. Rose, get me my soccer ball. Rose, bring me my laptop. Rose, I'm taking your cell phone. Rose, I'll have a Coke with crushed ice, not ice cubes. Hurry up, Rose.

And she had obeyed, loving every moment of his attention — even every moment of his lack of attention. And for what? So he could gang up against her when the whole reason for this was —

Rose righted herself. Even though ice cream cake was Tabor's idea of dessert and not hers, she might have some. "Tabor, back when it happened, I told everybody I didn't see anything. Which I didn't. And by now, it's so blank of a memory that I can't even truthfully say that I didn't see anything. I can only say I've forgotten."

There was silence.

"Sugarplum," said her father softly, "I could believe that if you hadn't destroyed the diary for all the days surrounding the murder."

"That's just coincidence," said Rose, and could have ripped her tongue out.

Her brother stared.

Her mother frowned, eyes white and glassy.

Her father went very still. "With what other event," he said carefully, "does the murder coincide?"

Why could she not remember a simple rule like silence?

Why couldn't it be bedtime?

Or better yet, next year?

"I can't understand why you have to analyze every syllable," she said hotly. "It's against the law to forget things?"

"Rose!" shouted her mother. "There is no reason for you to protect Milton Lofft! You start talking to us and you start *now*."

Rose hacked off a huge piece of cake, knew she couldn't swallow it, and set it back down.

"I assume," said her father, "that you really did witness the murder. So not only did you spend a weekend with a murderer, but you somehow cherish the experience and believe it should be protected. Rose, that is twisted and terrifying. I'm calling Ellen Klein and asking her to see you."

"Ellen Klein! Dad, that's Chrissie's mother! I cannot go see Ellen Klein. Anyway, she specializes in anorexia and self-mutilation. What will people think? If you send me to Mrs. Klein, I can't say anything to her, either, *because there isn't anything to say.*"

Sunday they went to church.

Tabor had no use for church, but for once he didn't say so, and Rose was relieved, because there was enough confrontation already.

The four Lymonds filled a pew, but none of their relatives were there. Lymonds had strong theological beliefs, so the Episcopalian Lymonds were irked by the

Baptist Lymonds, and the Presbyterian Lymonds held the Unitarian Lymonds in low regard. In a few hours, however, Nannie from her church, Mopsy and Popsy from theirs, Aunt Laura and her family, Uncle Matt and his family, the Wickham cousins and their steps would gather for Sunday brunch. The adults liked to compare sermons — unfavorably — and share gossip, of which they had a great deal, since among them, they saw everybody who attended any church at all.

Rose dreaded brunch. *She* was the gossip.

Any relative who had decided to sleep late, skip church, and forget brunch had changed his plans. Getting Rose's story would be the highlight of the week.

Her father's sweet tenor rang out on the first hymn and Tabor's baritone took the bottom line. "It's the only good thing about church," he whispered to his sister. "Four-part harmony."

It was certainly the only kind of harmony in Rose's family right now.

During the prayer of confession, Rose looked at her parents. Dad, of course, had a furrowed brow and cradled his head in his hands, probably agonizing about where he went wrong with Rose. Mom was serene, as though she had nothing on her conscience. This had always been the case. Whatever was said in prayer and sermon, Mom floated through, never considering that it might apply to her.

After church, they all got in the car and Mom said brightly, "I thought we'd go to that new Vietnamese restaurant. How does that sound?"

It sounded awful. Rose detested ethnic food. But she said nothing. She braced herself for the younger cousins — Caitlin, Oliver, Joel — who would pester her for details of cop cars and jails. For the older cousins — Grace, Morgan, Michael — who would not know how to treat her. For the aunts and uncles, trying to support Mom and Dad, but visibly glad their kids weren't behaving like Rose. For her grandparents, who would find Rose's every move appalling. For Nannie, who even more than Ming believed she should not get the silent treatment.

Inside the restaurant Rose felt blind. She couldn't see a single person she knew, let alone the Lymond hordes.

"Table for four?" asked the maître d'.

"Thank you," said her father, following him to a small booth in the back.

"Four?" said Rose, bewildered.

Her mother said, "It seemed easier, Rose."

The silver was wrapped in a heavy, starched pink napkin. Rose had difficulty extracting it without dropping it to the floor. She could hardly tell the fork from the spoon. She could hardly distinguish which end was the handle.

They're ashamed of me, she thought.

The secret, which had been inside her, swelled up and flourished, like some terrible external cancer.

Tabor was exhausted from the plane ride, the time changes, and the fact that he had not slept Saturday night, for worrying about what Rose knew. He could not remember ever being glad to attend church. But this morning, he had a feeling of safety. Whether it was being surrounded by family or the impossibility of further talk on dangerous subjects, church seemed truly to be a sanctuary.

The restaurant, however, was going to be torture. It certainly had not been chosen with Rose in mind, since her idea of good food was still a peanut butter sandwich.

In a dose of brotherly love that surprised him, Tabor took over the conversation. He talked easily, embroidering one story, enlarging on another, falsifying a third. His eyes came frequently to rest on his silent sister.

He tried to remember Rose four Novembers ago, but all that came to mind was how he despised her silly friends twittering like birds at a feeder over him and his friends. He couldn't remember what Rose looked like at twelve, just that he had not wanted her around. That had been the year of being musical. All he lived for that year was applause. He ached to impress other musicians, to impress a crowd, to impress a girl. He had not really noticed the girl who was his own sister.

Tabor watched Rose push food around on her plate. He knew she'd much rather have their usual brunch of French toast. He wanted, suddenly, to whisk his sister home, take her to the safety and comfort of ordinary food in their own ordinary kitchen.

Mom and Dad debated whether or not to have coffee, and whether or not the coffee should be decaf. Rose stared at them with a remote sadness that shocked Tabor.

She has a reason for silence, he thought.

He shivered.

CHAPTER ELEVEN

Anjelica Lofft was thinking about Rose. She could picture Rose as vividly as if they had just gotten together last week, but it had been four years.

From the time she was very small, Anjelica had brought girls home for the weekend because her parents were busy. If she didn't bring a friend, she had only the staff. The staff were generally nice, although rarely English-speaking. They never lasted long because the lake estate was isolated.

Depending on her father's interests at the moment, the staff would have specialties. At one time he had been in love with antique automobiles and that required two mechanics and a polisher. Three or four years ago, he'd sold most of the cars, having become interested in horses, and last spring he turned to gardens, formal European gardens that looked faintly ridiculous against the backdrop of rough mountains and choppy lake.

And yet, they didn't often go to the estate. Anjelica's mother didn't care for the country and would not have dreamed of getting on a horse. Cities were her passion and she liked to pick one every season.

The lake estate waited, baking in the sun or frosting in the snow, until the Loffts remembered to visit again.

There had been only one year when they went routinely to the lake estate. Anjelica was in seventh, her sole year in public school. Dad was vaguely thinking of running for office and had been advised that his only child couldn't be in private school if he wanted votes. But he lost interest in the political scene and soon Anjelica was back in private school.

What a relief when she was finally old enough for boarding school and Mother could travel all year and Dad could admit he cared for nothing but work.

But during the fall of seventh grade, Anjelica had been at a plain old public middle school. The building was impressively ugly, slabs of classrooms stacked at inconvenient angles. The student body, in Anjelica's opinion, closely resembled their school. They needed redesign and a better budget.

The girls traveled in packs. They were wrapped up in their own uninteresting world, as if their own little lives mattered; as if anybody cared.

Anjelica entertained herself by inviting only one member of a clique to the lake estate, and upon arrival she'd totally ignore the girl in order to demonstrate that nobody in dumb old middle school was desirable.

Her actual intent had been to show her parents a thing or two, but her parents did not notice. "How delightful to have you," they would say graciously to the little houseguest, and then they would vanish. Actually, it was usually Dad who vanished. Mother generally wasn't there to start with.

Perhaps she remembered Rose so clearly because Rose had not been interested in her, either. Rose had climbed into the car in a sort of stupor and was not roused by anything. When they arrived at the lake, Rose had hardly been able to find the front door, never mind notice whether Anjelica was in a room or out of it.

"She's like a grocery bag," Anjelica said to her father on that Saturday afternoon. "She's upright, she holds things, but that's all you can say of her." Anjelica had been worried about her father. He had not stopped pacing since they arrived at the mansion. He had the news playing on televisions throughout the house and kept going to the front door of the mansion, staring down the long, long drive that attached them to a remote mountain road.

What was he waiting for?

What did he want to know?

Who did he expect to appear?

"Just get through the weekend, Anjel," her father said tiredly. "On Monday we'll look for a good school, where the girls will measure up and be worthy of you." He flicked the remote and another news channel came up.

Sunday, having abandoned Rose for hours, Anjelica wandered back to see what the grocery bag was doing and found Rose writing page after page in a little leather-bound book.

Anjelica had to laugh.

A journal? How pathetic. Rose was lifeless. She could have nothing to write. But maybe Rose didn't think so. Maybe she was having a wonderful time. Maybe she was putting exclamation points after every sentence. Fun! Fun! Fun!

Anjelica dragged Rose outside, had the stable hands stick her on a horse, and sent them out for an hour. Rose bounced painfully and anxiously. Anjelica imagined her writing later in her journal, "Oooooh, I rode a horse! Anjelica has such a neat, neat, neat life. I'm sooooo lucky to be here."

Anjelica Lofft walked back to her house, dug through Rose's duffel bag, and took out the diary.

She read the entries at the back, and then she read them again. She had no idea how much time had passed, whether Rose had been out riding for ten minutes or two hours. The words on the page paralyzed her.

She almost cut out that page, but no matter how carefully Anjelica removed it, Rose would notice.

Anjelica Lofft was only twelve. She had never made an important decision by herself. How would her father handle this?

Milton Lofft loved to gamble. The higher the stakes, the more excited he got. Every aspect of his huge business was a gamble. That was what he and Frannie fought about. Frannie was careful; Milton Lofft despised being careful.

Anjelica gambled.

She gambled that Rose herself would destroy the diary. She gambled that nobody else would have a chance to glance at the diary — and if they did, Rose's secret would so appall them that they would have no eyes for other information.

The week following Rose's visit was hideous. The shock of Frannie's death was very great. Anjelica had been fond of Frannie. She grieved for months. She could still weep, wondering how frightened Frannie had been, how long it had taken, how much it had hurt.

Four years blurred her memory of Frannie but not of Rose. Whenever she thought of Rose, she shut her thoughts down. That memory had to be wrong.

Her father had been using the lake estate quite a bit this year, and many weekends Anjelica left boarding school to stay with him. Mother came more than once. It was nice to be a young woman with her parents instead of a kid.

When the police showed up at the lake estate wanting to discuss the murder of Frannie Bailey, Anjelica was stunned. Surely they had given up, stuck the paper file in some storeroom and the computer file on some unused disk.

Her father did not allow her to be present for the questioning, nor did he allow them to question her. Afterward she said, "What did they ask about?"

He shrugged. "Same as before. Was Frannie alive when I left. They actually implied that I'm paying the Lymond child off. Buying her silence. Can you imagine? I told them to check her bank accounts. Then they implied that the girl herself had something to do with Frannie's death. I said, Don't be insane, she was just a little kid! Leave the poor girl alone."

Dad went back to work, visibly unworried. His computer sucked him in, because for Milton Lofft, the world was virtual and the screen was real.

But the police came back.

It was only two weekends later.

Her father was in his office, dealing with business problems in Asia. Dad would not have let the police in a second time, but Anjelica was desperate to know what had made them reopen the case. "What else is there to ask?" she said, trying to look mildly puzzled instead of frantic.

The police said, "Is your father here? Would you ask him to join us?"

"Certainly." Anjelica's knees were shaking. She left them in the vast stone foyer and walked down a long, sweeping corridor to Dad's office. A wall of windows faced the mountains while the interior wall was lined with the sculptures Dad bought the year he was interested in Mayan culture.

But in his office, Dad burst out laughing. "The funniest thing," he said. "I meant to tell you, Anjel. That little girl — Rose Lymond, remember? — she kept a diary. My attorneys found out about it. They called me the other day."

Anjelica Lofft had lost her gamble. Rose Lymond had not thrown away the diary.

It had had little hot watercolors on each page; flowers in scarlet or leaves in orange. Rose's neat, curly script had disintegrated toward the end and she had not even seen the illustrations but written right over them.

How could her father be laughing? Unless Anjelica was wrong about what she had read. Or Rose had been wrong when she wrote.

"The Lymond kid was so worried the police would read it," said Milton Lofft, "that she actually stole the police car where they'd put her diary. Is that crazy or what? I still remember you called her a grocery bag. I loved that phrase, Anjel. You've always been so good with words."

It was Rose's words that were going to count now. Anjelica couldn't even breathe. She felt as if she had asthma. In seventh grade there had even been a little girl who died of asthma. Middle school and memory closed in on Anjelica. She was sick with anxiety.

"So then," said Anjelica's father, "the kid rips up the pages and flushes them down the toilet in some Burger King. I'd hire this Lymond girl in a heartbeat. She doesn't fool around. I bet the police won't tell me they never read the diary." He got up from his computer screen. "I bet they've come to imply that in her diary, Rose Lymond tells all."

Anjelica walked dazedly after her father, who entertained himself by stonewalling the police. He was good at it. By the end of the twenty minutes he allotted for this, Anjelica had decided that the police had no shiny new piece of evidence. The case had been reopened for splash value. Milton Lofft was a big fish. Be a kick to reel him in. The police were dangling a worm in the water to see if anything bit.

But it was Rose Lymond who had bitten when she destroyed her diary.

In a sense, therefore, Anjelica Lofft was free. The entries were gone as if they had never been. She could set her worry down.

But Anjelica was no longer twelve. She was sixteen. Her worries were older and heavier, and her need to know was far more acute. What had Rose Lymond actually seen?

It doesn't matter, Anjelica told herself a thousand times.

It does matter, she said another thousand.

Anjelica called her boarding school to say that she was ill and would return a day late. She took a spare car and drove ninety miles south to the city, past the house they had once lived in and the ugly middle school.

What a selfish little rat she had been at age twelve.

She imagined herself showing up at high school, running into the girls she had treated so badly in seventh. It was not a pleasant thought.

I've turned out quite well, she told them silently. You might even like me now. I'm nice a good deal of the time and make an effort to be kind. I'm hardly ever sarcastic and now I know what it is to fail, and be unpopular, and get hurt.

She ate in a restaurant even Mother had thought

adequate. From there she telephoned Rose's friend Chrissie. That had been stupid.

Twice she tried to talk to Rose. Also stupid.

Anjelica had to laugh when she thought of Rose.

She and Rose were blundering down the exact same path, saving their secrets, maintaining their silence.

On Monday after school, Alan Finney was aware the moment Rose Lymond joined the small crowd on the bleachers on the west side of the baseball diamond. Baseball always gave you time to look around. The sunny, slow pace of baseball never failed to seduce him. It was a game that could explode at the crack of a bat or drift aimlessly, inning after inning.

He was not surprised to see Rose.

The Lymonds were big sports fans. They followed high school sports, local minor league teams, and distant major league teams. They followed baseball and basketball, football and golf, soccer and tennis. He had the impression that Rose attended games because her father did. She liked being with her father.

Alan liked being with his father, too, but Alan's father had a long commute and a demanding job and wasn't around much. Rose's father got to more games than Alan's, and Mr. Lymond didn't even have a kid playing this year.

Now that he knew Rose was in the crowd, Alan stopped looking at the crowd. If he let himself think about Rose, he wouldn't be able to play.

Tabor had called Alan a second time. "Stop her from doing anything dumb, Alan," he'd said anxiously.

Rose isn't the one doing anything, thought Alan.

But to Tabor, he said, "Okay. I'll keep an eye on her."

It was obvious to Chrissie that Rose did not know what she was doing. And it was possible that the Loffts did.

So Monday after school, Chrissie told her coach she'd be late for practice.

"You'll what? You will not! You will —"

But by chance, Mr. Burgess, the vice principal, was passing by.

"I'm behind in my research," said Chrissie loudly, looking down on her five-foot-seven coach. "I have to spend an hour in the library or fail."

Her coach didn't give a fried doughnut whether Chrissie failed but could hardly say so in front of Mr. Burgess. Smiling falsely at both of them, Chrissie left fast, before the situation changed.

The school library was silent except for the clicking of keys, the humming of printers, and the churning out of paper. Nobody looked at anybody, being far too involved with their screens. At hers, Chrissie pulled up the local newspaper and keyed in the school account to pay for access. In moments, she had found that November of four years ago.

The Friday morning paper would have been printed

and distributed by dawn, twelve hours before Rose was picked up by Milton Lofft. It was the Saturday regional section that would actually tell what had happened on Friday.

Darn little.

OFFICIALS WANT SECOND OPINION ON COST OF NEW ELEMENTARY SCHOOL

Well, they never had built the new elementary school, so presumably the second opinion had been negative.

SENIORS FACE MAZE OF HEALTH CARE OPTIONS

Chrissie found herself unable to worry.

TOWN BOARD HAS VACANCY

It turned out to be the Wetlands Commission. There were times when Chrissie worried that being an adult was going to be boring.

SPRAY TREATMENT SUGGESTED FOR MOSQUITOES

BOARD OF REC OFFERS TRIP TO NEW YORK

HIT-AND-RUN ENDS LIFE

This looked promising. She read the sad little article carefully. The newspaper thoughtfully printed a map to show where the fatality had happened. But nobody on this side of the city would drive over there; too many good malls and movie theaters a lot closer.

She read on.

Sunday and Monday were especially boring days in state and local history.

Tuesday, at last, the paper covered the murder.

Chrissie settled in.

Frannie Bailey had been Milton Lofft's partner for ten years. The two of them had developed financial programs for personal computers, and Frannie Bailey's net worth was estimated at a hundred fifty million, which didn't seem too shabby to Chrissie.

Frannie Bailey had been gardening just before her death. Her sneakers and trousers were earth-stained and her fingernails rimmed with dirt.

What gardening did you do in November? Chrissie wondered. Did you plant bulbs, dreaming of spring? Had Frannie Bailey been thinking of tulips when she died?

The victim had been hit over the head with a rock from her garden, said the article. Time of death would be determined by autopsy.

There were interviews, of course.

Milton Lofft expressed shock and dismay. He had seen his partner Friday afternoon and she had been fine. He had not gone inside the house but yelled through an open window.

When asked why he had not gone inside to talk, Milton Lofft replied that he never went in. Asked why he hadn't used his computer to send the information on one of his own encrypted programs, he said he needed Frannie Bailey's immediate response. Asked why he didn't call on his car phone, he said he had been bringing her something.

Asked what, he replied, Not your business.

Further questions were not answered.

In Wednesday's paper, neighbors said that Milton Lofft and Frannie Bailey frequently had screaming arguments, he standing in the drive, she leaning out an upstairs window. It seemed to be the way they conducted business.

Police questioned business associates, the garbagemen, postman, FedEx driver, the boy who mowed the lawn, and the girl who walked the dogs. No useful information was obtained.

Thursday, the police questioned little Anjelica Lofft and her friend, unidentified, who had been waiting in the car during the argument between Milton Lofft and Frannie Bailey. Neither girl had seen anything.

Great, thought Chrissie. I don't see anything, either. My coach hates me and I learned nothing.

She went into the newspaper's index and typed "milton lofft," which produced several hundred hits. Forget it. She typed in "anjelica lofft" and this produced only one. The article took forever to appear.

It was a recent photograph with a caption. It showed Milton Lofft standing near an elevator with his daughter and a slew of computer giants and their daughters. Take Your Daughter to Work Day. Who would have expected Anjelica Lofft to participate in something so ordinary?

Anjelica was far more attractive than Chrissie remembered. Angular and bony, just right to model clothes but not soft enough to model makeup.

Chrissie shut down the computer, whose little icons

vanished inside the screen as Frannie Bailey had vanished from life. Completely.

But icons could be resurrected and Frannie Bailey was not coming back to tell what had happened.

Rose watched Alan play. There was something perfect about a ball game: the combination of sky, grass, and diamond; the speed of the pitch and the swing of the bat.

At the bottom of the eighth, the score even, she found herself unable to tolerate the pressure. She decided to walk to Nannie's and play croquet. There was a ladylike violence to croquet, the sound of two hard balls hitting, like skulls.

The grass under her feet was soft and bouncy, like the grass in her yard. She was relieved when she reached the road.

She pictured Nannie in a yellow cotton dress and wide-brimmed straw hat with ribbons. She heard Nannie boast, "Guess what movie I rented for us! Don't tell your father, of course. I saw it last year. We'll scream through the whole thing."

Oh, Nannie! thought Rose. What do I do?

Rose walked on and on. She detested exercise that didn't count. She liked a coach giving her credit, or a Stairmaster registering her efforts, or at least a friend at her side who could be out of breath before she was. Yet she stretched the walk out, dawdling and leaning on things and wasting time, the way she had walked home from the Y four years ago, filled with silly airy daydreams about the lovely popular time at Anjelica's. Worrying about what suitcase or duffel to use. As if it would matter, in the end.

Rose wondered if she'd ever be allowed to drive or if she was doomed to walking for the rest of her life. Nannie of course had not been allowed to drive for years. Nannie said it was criminal, the way her grown sons had ripped her car out of her life, turning her into a recluse and destroying all her fun. "Better than destroying stray cats or three-year-olds," Dad explained.

Nannie was not amused. "I have never had an accident in my life," she said fiercely.

Not that you noticed, thought Rose.

She was hot, and the walk made her hotter, and it felt as if she might go on and on, walking, walking, walking, and never arriving. On her right was the town cemetery, stone after stone, and the grave markers seemed to walk beside her, agreeing that she would never arrive. Under old trees bloomed lily of the valley, scenting the air like a wedding or a funeral.

A car roared. It sounded close enough to drive up her spine. It was losing control, brutally tearing tire tracks in the soft grass. It was mowing her down.

Rose flung herself into the cemetery. Her face missed a headstone by inches; she caught her elbow on it and skinned both knees painfully under her jeans.

But when she looked back, the vehicle was not out of control and had not torn up the grass. Her imagination was the thing killing her.

"Sorry, Rose," said Alan Finney, leaning out the window of his black Explorer. He was still in his baseball uniform, sweaty and grimy. "I didn't mean to startle you."

She got up, determined not to let him realize that she had hurt herself. "You drive too fast, Alan."

"I happen to be an excellent driver."

"You're a terrible driver. Look at all the daffodils you just mashed." People didn't mind if you said they were terrible at math or art or catching a ball. But tell them they were a bad driver and you stabbed them through the heart. She cradled her hurt elbow, studying Alan's transportation. The Explorer was your basic boxy anonymous sports utility vehicle.

Suppose it was Alan who tried to run over me, she thought. Then I've been really wrong about somebody. Of course the whole problem here is how wrong I've been about people.

"Where are you going?" asked Alan.

"Nannie's," she said. "How come you didn't stay to shower? Who won? Where are *you* going?"

"I need to talk to you," he said. "Coach let me go early. We won by one. Hop in. We need to talk. Please?"

She got in. Her feet got tangled in his school backpack, laptop carrier, pizza box, CD container, and unzipped, overflowing sports duffel.

Memory returned so hard and fast she needed steel shutters against the hurricane of it. Coming in the door to hear Mom and Aunt Sheila chatting, Aunt Sheila saying, "Of course I haven't seen Rose in five years so I was holding my breath."

She remembered the crazed frantic need to write. Her hand clenching the pencil, her grip so tight her hands ached all night. Alan's fingers seemed to be that tight on his steering wheel.

"There's the turn to Nannie's, Alan."

For a moment, she thought Alan was going to drive past. That he did have somewhere to go, and she wouldn't have liked it. In his face was indecision that was close to fear. But he turned in, and there was Nannie, garden shears in her hand, going after a blue hyacinth.

Nannie's yard was big and run-down, with overgrown lilacs looming over porches and a fifty-year-old swing set rusting in the back. The house itself looked too small for raising a family, but here Nannie had had four children, and now eleven great-grandchildren.

If that was the right number.

Nannie straightened, one hand pushing at her spine to accomplish it.

"It's me, Rose, Nannie," she called, so that her great-grandmother would not be worried about a strange car. Whatever it was he needed to say, Alan hadn't said it yet, so Rose offered him time. "Want to stay, Alan? We'll play croquet. Nannie's good. She'll whip us both."

Alan looked at Rose as if there were a smudged window between them and he could not see her clearly. "I'd like that," he said slowly, and he stayed, and the three of them played croquet, and Great-grandmother Nannie Lymond flirted madly with a boy sixty-eight years younger. She actually made Alan blush.

Although he claimed never to have played croquet, Alan got into the spirit of the game, whacking Rose's ball so far out of bounds that Rose had to cross a brook to get it back.

"You killed her," said Nannie with satisfaction.

Alan caught his breath and looked away.

CHAPTER TWELVE

Chrissie Klein was taking a geometry test. She was having no trouble with the equations. There was time to glance out the window and dream of summer and getting older and possibly even taller. Beyond a row of flowering dogwoods, a gray Pathfinder circled slowly among the hundreds of student cars in their slanting slots, looking for a space. Somebody was seriously late for class.

The driver got out, a tall, slim girl wearing khaki pants and a plain navy tee, hair pulled into a ponytail. The girl blended well against the spring watercolor of the trees. Chrissie watched her thread through the packed parking lot, heading for the front lobby.

It was Anjelica Lofft.

Chrissie's hair prickled.

What could Anjelica be here for? Why wasn't she attending her own school? Surely even boarding school did not end this early in the spring. Was she cutting class to be here? What information could be in the office that Anjelica Lofft needed? The same information she would have asked Chrissie for, if Chrissie had stayed on the phone? And if Anjelica didn't want information, why visit? The high school was filled with the same kids she had despised four years ago.

Or was Anjelica meeting somebody? In which case, who on earth had remained friends with her?

Rose?

Chrissie berated herself for not forcing the Anjelica issue after all. She had let school and sports and food take precedence over the Rose problem. She glanced at the clock. One more minute and this class would be over. She'd better find Rose during passing period. "Hey, Halsey," she muttered. "Where's Rose right now? And what's her next class?"

Halsey shrugged and kept working.

Keith whispered, "She has art this period, I think."

"Time's up, pass papers forward," said the math teacher.

Halsey sighed, passed hers forward, and said, "Next, Rose has history, Room 202. I know because I do, too. We have a test there as well. I wrecked this one, I'll probably wreck that one, Rose will get extra credit and score a hundred and ten."

Chrissie couldn't care less how Halsey did on quizzes. She gathered her stuff and hurried. Art was in its own wing, next to drama and across from music.

She didn't want Rose having to deal with Anjelica Lofft right now. Anjelica was about as sensitive as a sidewalk. How disappointing Anjelica's choice of car was. A girl with so much money should at least be in a Lexus.

A thousand students flooded the halls, swinging

book bags, stopping at lockers, getting drinks of water, rushing into bathrooms, exchanging news, continuing classroom arguments. Chrissie had never seen so many people she did not care about.

She did not find Rose.

Art was empty.

Chrissie turned around and walked all the way back to 202, and by the time she arrived, history class had already begun and she was going to be very late for her own. "Rose here?" she asked.

"Ought to be," said the teacher, looking around.

But Rose was not there.

"Rose cutting class," said one of the boys. "It's the same sad story, isn't it? First you steal a police car — next, you skip history."

The class laughed. Chrissie did not.

It isn't *first steal a police car*, she thought. It's *first see something the Loffts don't want you to see*.

Chrissie broke into a run.

The map in the newspaper article finally made sense.

She sped toward the office before realizing that Rose, who had had the guts to steal a police car, would not bother with authority. Chrissie swerved, picking the nearest exit to the student parking lot.

She knew what the second secret was.

Rose was astonished to find herself next to Anjelica Lofft. They walked companionably, matching pace in the sea of students changing classes. "I hardly recognized you, Anjelica," said Rose, as disoriented as if Nannie had appeared in a yellow frock, swinging a red croquet mallet.

"I hardly recognized *you*. You look *wonderful*," said Anjelica. Rose must have looked so awful in seventh that Anjelica had very low expectations for her in tenth.

How had Anjelica gotten into the building? There was supposed to be a floor monitor who ID'd guests and strangers. This was ridiculous, of course, since there were a thousand kids in the school. No hall monitor knew all of them. Anjelica need only melt into the crowd. And she had.

"Rose," said Anjelica, "will you cut a class and come for a drive with me? We need to talk. Or at least I need to talk. I know you have the answers."

Answers? To what questions?

What could possibly matter to Anjelica?

Only if Anjelica's father really and truly had killed Frannie Bailey could Anjelica have a reason for wanting Rose to answer questions. But Rose knew nothing about that murder; she never had; she had always taken the same stance and said the same things. Anjelica had been there. The two girls were in agreement. They had seen nothing.

Alan had said the same thing, though. *We need to talk.*

Why would Rose need to talk to either of them?

Why would they need to talk to her?

"Just ten minutes, Rose, please?" said Anjelica. She looked tired and drawn. "Fifteen at the most. We'll slip out the side door. We'll sit in my car and talk."

Rose felt her silence slipping away, her grip on saying nothing growing slack and weak. How strange and awful, if she were to admit her secret to Anjelica, a stranger who had barely shown basic friendliness, never mind depth of heart. But she never cut class and next was history, which she loved, and talking with Anjelica could only be unpleasant. She shook her head no.

"Rose," said Anjelica, "I read your diary. I read it when you went riding with the stable hands, just before my father and I drove you back to your house. I read every word you wrote."

Alan Finney was sitting in European history.

Because Alan hated studying and had several hundred more interesting things to do, he paid close attention in class, so as to avoid the subject again in the evening.

The history teacher had gotten stranded on the Napoleonic Wars, where she lingered long and lovingly. This left her barely a month of the school year into which she must squash two hundred years of history. It was not going well. Wars, peace treaties, prime ministers, empires, and navies slammed into one another and raced on into the next generation.

Alan stared out the window, which he never permitted himself to do, because views out the window were too satisfying. Start gazing out windows, you started to go deaf to the lecture, and then you had to study at home.

Out the window, Alan saw Rose Lymond and Anjelica Lofft walking toward the student parking lot.

He recognized Anjelica because she had been featured in a teen magazine a year ago, and of all people, Tabor had bought the magazine and shown the pictures around. Anjelica was beautiful and rich, but so were lots of girls. The difference was that the boys had a tiny association with Anjelica; the band had kicked her out of the Lymonds' cellar the day she came to play with Rose.

What a sweet phrase: to play with Rose. It conjured up happy, smiling children pretending to ride ponies or explore rain forests. But there could be nothing sweet about Anjelica Lofft coaxing Rose Lymond to leave the high school with her.

In his second phone call, Tabor had told Alan about the attempted hit-and-run during Rose's trash detail. "What could it be about?" Tabor had moaned. "Who would try to hit my sister with his car? And why would she lie about it?"

European history cluttered Alan's mind. The breathing and fidgeting and muttering of the class, the scrape of pencils and the click of laptops offended him, chewed at his thoughts.

Who *would* try to run Rose over? thought Alan. It must be a Lofft. And maybe it isn't Milton who would like to run Rose down. Maybe it's Anjelica.

He tilted his chair back to keep Rose in sight as the two girls crossed the parking lot and then the parking lot itself tipped Alan's memory. All those cars. All the traffic and all the tie-ups that knotted the roads around the school every day at two forty-five. Kids gunning their engines, jumping the lights, passing on the right even if it meant driving on lawns or crushing innocent shrubs.

Passing on the right, thought Alan.

He stood up way too fast, something he was usually careful not to do because he was too large for the desks and chairs in the high school classrooms. He kicked over his desk and nearly tripped over this chair.

"Alan," said the teacher.

"Sorry," he said, stepping over backpacks and book bags and purses and legs. "I'll explain later." Which was a lie. He wasn't going to explain a single thing later.

In the hall, he broke into a sprint.

Rose had written quite a lot about traffic, even though traffic had not been on her mind at all. Alan bet traffic wasn't on her mind now, either.

The diary sprang into his mind as if a printer spewed out the pages.

I didn't think we'd ever get to the lake estate. Even after we got on the thruway we had sixty miles to go. I was desperate to crawl into a bed and pull the covers over my head. Maybe in the morning it would turn out to be a bad dream. I was so upset and the drive lasted forever. Anjelica kept opening bags of chips and Mr. Lofft was furious at the traffic. We hit something and bumped over it and it felt as if the Navigator would tip over. Anjelica screamed and her own father swore at her.

My soul has hit something and bumped over it. Every breath I take, I'm going over another bump. But it's morning as I write this, and it wasn't a bad dream, and it isn't a bump I can drive over.

There is a second secret, thought Alan. The bump in the road when Milton Lofft passed on the right. It's the hit-and-run. The one the police accused me of. Accused Tabor of and even the whole band of.

The police were half right about everything. Milton Lofft is guilty of murder. Just not the murder of Frannie Bailey.

We'll probably never know who murdered Frannie Bailey. Rose told the truth: Neither she nor Anjelica saw anything at Frannie Bailey's house.

But both of them felt the bump when Milton Lofft drove over a pedestrian and kept going. Anjelica screamed. She probably actually saw it. Rose didn't scream so she probably only felt it. I don't suppose Rose even knows she wrote about the hit-and-run. She might not even know that any hit-and-run ever happened.

But Anjelica knows because, of course, she read the diary, too. Rose must have been writing the entire weekend, pouring out her shock. How furious it would make a Lofft to be ignored in favor of some stupid diary. Anjelica sneaked a peek the way I did.

So the person who tried to run Rose over on trash detail was Anjelica herself. She has to protect her father, thought Alan. Anjelica knew that, sooner or later, Rose would break down and talk. One good interrogation and out that sentence would come: *We hit something and bumped over it and it felt as if the Navigator would tip over.*

Turning the first corner, Alan nearly crushed Chrissie Klein racing toward the same exit.

"Rose!" said Chrissie.

"With Anjelica," agreed Alan.

Chrissie reached the door first and flung it open. "Did you read the diary?" she panted.

"Yes."

"Scum."

"Did you read it?" he demanded. "That makes you scum, too."

"Yes," said Chrissie, "but I've never denied being scum."

Alan caught the door and they were outside and the air was sweet and mild after the stale recirculated air of the school.

"Talk about scum," said Alan, pointing. "Anjelica's driving out the back way. We can't signal Rose. We're not going to get there in time."

"Do you have your car?"

"Yes."

"We'll follow them," said Chrissie.

They flew to Alan's car, leaped in, fastened seat belts, drove away leaving a patch, and got caught by traffic at the first intersection. The wait for lights to change was excruciating. "I bet Rose wouldn't hang around like this," said Chrissie. "Rose would just steal a quicker car and get going."

They both laughed hysterically. The image of Rose in a stolen vehicle remained impossible.

At last they were through the intersection and speeding after Anjelica's almost vanished Pathfinder. Alan was an excellent driver, taking extreme risks and going very fast, just like Tabor. Anjelica swung an abrupt left, forcing Alan to change lanes between two speeding semis. Chrissie was very respectful.

There were several gray cars ahead of them now. She was not sure which was Anjelica's.

"It adds up to Milton Lofft being the driver in that hit-and-run," said Alan.

"I saw the map when I read the old newspapers," agreed Chrissie, "but I was too stupid to figure out that if Milton Lofft drove to Frannie Bailey's, he'd be getting back on the turnpike way over there, so I didn't pay attention to it."

The light turned. The Explorer ripped forward. Far ahead of them, Anjelica was turning left near a McDonald's arches.

"I think being a driver in a hit-and-run runs in the Lofft family," Alan said.

"What do you mean by that?"

"The first day Rose had trash detail out on I-395, some car tried to run over her. It was probably Anjelica."

Chrissie was shocked. She had not known. What else hadn't Rose told her? But we haven't been close in so long, she thought. Why should Rose tell me anything?

"But," said Chrissie, "Rose didn't write in her diary that she saw Milton Lofft run over an innocent pedestrian and keep going. She wrote that she felt a bump one block before a thruway entrance. The police can't use that against Milton Lofft. Rose herself doesn't even remember it. One line in a diary that doesn't even exist anymore is not proof. So why would Anjelica be worried enough to run Rose over?"

But Alan was not listening to Chrissie. He was gripping the steering wheel even harder, shaken by a new thought. "A few days ago, Rose was walking to her great-grandmother's. She freaked out when I pulled over to give her a ride. I thought she was afraid of Milton Lofft. But, Chrissie, she was afraid of *me*. Rose thought *I* was the one who tried to run her down. She even thought I was trying again."

"Don't be silly," said Chrissie, who now immediately thought of Alan and whether *he* could be the bad guy.

Maybe Anjelica is *saving* Rose, thought Chrissie. But from whom?

CHAPTER THIRTEEN

njelica turned into the drive-through lane of the McDonald's. This did not seem like the act of a desperate killer. Although presumably even desperate killers got hungry.

Alan yanked his car between traffic to enter McDonald's, rudely inserting himself in front of cars that deserved to be ahead of him and pulling up behind Anjelica so fast and so hard Chrissie was afraid they'd hit the Pathfinder. Alan released his seat belt, threw open the door, and raced to Anjelica, bending into her side window, which was down because she had just placed her order.

Anjelica was so startled she nearly drove through the car ahead of her.

But Alan was much more startled.

Anjelica Lofft was alone in her car.

Chrissie flung open her own door, leaped out, and raced to the passenger side of Anjelica's car, ready to rescue Rose. The passenger seat was empty. Alan, gaping through Anjelica's window, and Chrissie, gaping through the passenger side, stared at each other across Anjelica's very annoyed face.

"Where is Rose?" yelled Chrissie.

The car behind Alan honked irritably, since his abandoned Explorer now blocked any future food order. Alan waved. The driver was not pacified but honked louder.

Anjelica glared at each of them in turn. "Who are you? Get your stupid heads out of my car."

"Alan Finney," said Alan.

"Chrissie Klein," said Chrissie.

Anjelica's jaw dropped. They had truly astonished her. Chrissie watched as Anjelica stacked Chrissie's twelve-year-old self and Alan's fourteen-year-old self against what they had become. It seemed to amuse her. "This better be good," she said. "Get out from under my tires. I'll pull into a parking space."

Embarrassed and puzzled, Alan returned to the Explorer and found an empty space to park it in. Anjelica pulled out of the drive-through line and drove up next to him but did not get out.

Once more, Chrissie and Alan flanked her, stooping to look through her open windows. This time, Anjelica seemed neither hostile nor amused, just tired. She traced the circle of her steering wheel with her fingers.

"Where is Rose?" said Chrissie meekly.

Anjelica shrugged. "She was going to come for a drive with me, because I wanted to talk, but some man came up to us and asked her to go with him instead. So she did."

They were dumbfounded.

Alan had just been thinking that somehow he and

Chrissie had not spotted Rose quietly returning to school as Anjelica drove out the back. He felt like a fool. Maybe he and Chrissie could think up a good lie to explain themselves or maybe, like Rose, they should decide on silence. For whom would Rose Lymond cut school?

"Was it a cop?" asked Chrissie.

"I don't think so," said Anjelica. "Not in uniform, anyway."

"Her brother, maybe?" Alan said, confusedly. "Tabor?"

"No, I would have recognized Tabor."

"Then who was it?"

Anjelica shrugged again. "He didn't say his name."

"You can't just shrug this off!" snapped Chrissie.

"Why are you so worked up?" said Anjelica.

"Rose's life is in danger."

Anjelica seemed genuinely irritated. "Don't be silly."

"Anjelica," said Chrissie intensely, as if they still had classes together, and lunch, and long, intimate talks on the telephone. As if they were friends. "Somebody tried to kill Rose. They tried to run her over."

Anjelica paled. Against the dark upholstery of her car, she seemed ghostlike and shrunken. "I don't believe you," she whispered. She tried to lick her lips but her tongue had dried, and she was breathing hard.

"We thought it was you," said Chrissie.

Anjelica stared at her in horror. Then she shook her head.

Chrissie and Alan stood helplessly, the secrets they

had not known after all swirling between them. The truth was as elusive as it had been that Friday four years ago.

And Rose — Rose had vanished with a stranger. The only other man in the case was Milton Lofft, and it could not be Milton Lofft with whom Rose had driven away.

"Tell us about the guy," said Alan.

"Early twenties. Blue jeans and a sweatshirt. Nothing much to look at."

Neither Chrissie nor Alan had any idea who it might be.

"Why did you want to talk to Rose, anyway?" asked Chrissie, no longer sure that she knew.

The bones of Anjelica's face stood out like a preliminary drawing for a painting. "Stealing a police car," she said finally. "It's rather amazing, don't you think? Why didn't Rose just take the diary back from the police and refuse to turn it over to them again? She would have been within her rights. Anything she didn't want them to read, she could have gotten rid of in a sensible, quiet way. Stealing a police car? Tell me that didn't knock your socks off."

"Yes," said Chrissie.

"I wanted to understand," said Anjelica slowly. "I was part of her life for a moment and it turns out to have been a very important moment. So I drove down here, thinking we would talk. She wasn't enthusiastic about spending time with me, but she didn't refuse. We were halfway across the parking lot when the man came up and she seized on the excuse to go with him instead. She knew him. She said hello first. She was surprised and pleased to see him."

Surprised and pleased, thought Alan. Who could this be? "Did she say his name?"

"I had the impression Rose couldn't remember his name. That she knew him once, or knew him when he was a kid and he'd changed. He said to her, 'Tabor's rearranged his final exams and he's coming home early. He wants to sort things out. We're meeting him at the airport.'"

Alan's skin crawled. Was he totally wrong about Milton Lofft being the driver of the hit-and-run? Could the driver in the hit-and-run have been this unknown man? Could the driver have been *Tabor*? What if *Tabor* had run somebody over and driven away and pretended to be elsewhere? Rose would protect Tabor from anything. But whose car would Tabor have been driving? He hadn't owned a car four years ago. This unknown man's car? Four years ago, who had they all known who owned a car? That Rose would be surprised and pleased to see again?

But Anjelica had lost interest. "Now I have to go inside to get my order," she snapped. "I hate going inside. This is your fault." She grabbed her purse, opened her door, making Alan step back, and stalked to the side entrance.

"That was just an excuse," said Chrissie. "She doesn't care about food. She just wanted to get away from us before we asked more questions."

"I'm too stupid to think of more questions," said Alan.

They sat in his Explorer. The windshield glass had magnified the sun and the car was toasty.

"I've got Tabor's beeper number," said Alan finally. "He gave it to me the other day when he called to tell me to keep an eye on Rose."

They used Chrissie's cell phone to call Tabor.

Anjelica came back out of the restaurant. Her little brown paper bag smelled deliciously of salt and grease. Chrissie truly had no idea if Anjelica was friend or foe. She tried to imagine somebody attempting to kill Rose on the highway. She even tried to imagine a *third* secret, one that none of them had figured out.

"Who were you phoning?" said Anjelica. This time she was the one standing on the pavement looking in the car window and waiting for information.

"Tabor. You might as well sit with us while we wait for him to call back," said Alan ungraciously. "Get in."

She got in the back. "Your entire car is a trash can, Alan."

"I don't have servants to vacuum it. And you're not driving much of a car at all. What's with the Pathfinder? Your suburban disguise?"

Anjelica went red. Then she shrugged. "You're right. I usually drive a Boxster. I borrowed this."

They sat uncomfortably.

Alan yearned to know what color her Boxster was but he forced himself not to ask. He yearned to have some of her French fries, too, but he gritted his teeth and played with the steering wheel instead.

It was another five minutes before Tabor called. "Chrissie Klein?" he was shouting in horror. "Chrissie! What's going on? Why are you calling me? What's happened to my sister?"

"It's me, Alan," said Alan. "I forgot Chrissie's name would come up on your beeper. Sorry. Just tell me if you're catching a plane and coming home early."

"No," said Tabor.

Alan filled him in. "Who could this guy be, Tabor?"

Tabor was still breathing hard from anxiety. "He's got to be somebody I know pretty well, or Rose wouldn't believe he's the one meeting me at the airport. But I can't think of anybody."

Chrissie felt as tense as if they were in the last ten seconds of a tied game. And she had to make the bucket or they'd lose. In this case, Rose would lose. "It's not good," said Chrissie, "that the guy lied about why Rose should go with him. Listen, Anjelica. What kind of car was it?"

"Sports utility vehicle of some kind. I think a dark color. I didn't really look. I was upset and I felt stupid and I just wanted to get away and pretend I hadn't tried to talk to her in the first place."

Chrissie thought, Anjelica borrows cars. She could probably borrow a killer, too. Maybe we were right about the second secret. Maybe Anjelica is still trying to protect her father. And here we sit, giving her an alibi while her hired hand gets rid of Rose.

Except — Rose knew the guy.
Who is it?

Rose still had not thought of his name.

Okay, she said to herself, he was the founding member of Tabor's band. He didn't stay long. He was — who was he? He's — he's —

"Verne," she said out loud, beaming at him, relieved to have remembered.

He was not good-looking, although Halsey and Erin had thought him terrific at the time. Perhaps it had been just age; perhaps eighteen was so beautiful to a twelve-year-old that it needed nothing more. Perhaps with his guitar and his driver's license, he had seemed the pinnacle of manliness.

Rose hadn't known that Verne and Tabor were still in touch. It did not surprise her, however, that Tabor would change his finals. He was probably in danger of failing something and Tabor was adept at excusing himself from difficult tasks. What a great reason to peddle to a professor — a sister who desperately needed him at home.

Since Mom and Dad couldn't afford to fly Tabor in again so soon, how was he paying for this?

He must have a job, she thought, and he's actually saved the money himself! Dad will be so proud. He loves it when his kids manage money well. It doesn't happen often.

She settled in for the ride to the airport. It was a relief not to have to talk to Anjelica after all. Rose had obediently written down Anjelica's beeper number and car phone number and maybe she would call one day, because Anjelica had not seemed threatening, but sad and lost. What could beat down Anjelica Lofft?

Verne left the school parking lot behind and turned toward the city. The airport was out in the country, miles from here. She wondered what they could talk about for such a long drive. She couldn't remember where Verne went to college. Or if. Verne had faded toward the end of his senior year, as if he'd used himself up already. "How's school?" she said, hoping for a clue.

"School is fine," said Verne. He gave her an exceptionally happy smile. She didn't know what to make of it.

"Where is it you're going now?" she asked.

"The airport."

She laughed. "I mean, which college?"

He shrugged.

"You dropped out?" she said anxiously. Parents were so disappointed and angry if their children dropped out of college. She couldn't remember Verne's parents. Had they ever come when the band played? They must have.

Verne adjusted the volume of the music he was playing on the car radio, but instead of turning it down low enough for conversation, he hiked it so high that the car vibrated. Rose's head hurt from the assault of heavy metal. He turned the bass up even more, until the drums seemed to beat on Rose's skull.

She pressed her hands to her temples and the volume of many voices roared in her ears, and most of all, the volume of Aunt Sheila's voice.

For four years, Rose had turned that volume down, until Aunt Sheila dwindled into nothing, and Rose could not hear those terrible words. Now, as if sneering inside the pounding scream of Verne's tape, the bass spiked up until it controlled Rose's heartbeat, and Aunt Sheila's words blared forth.

"Of course I haven't seen Rose in five years," said Aunt Sheila, "so I was holding my breath. How would she turn out? You are so lucky, Julia. A person could pretend Rose looks like Tommy."

"Tommy thinks Rose does look like him," agreed Mom. "Tommy likes to say Rose is just like her great-grandmother."

The sisters, Julia and Sheila, laughed.

Rose, in the hall, inches from the final step into the kitchen, did not laugh.

"It must have been such a relief to you when Bruce moved away," said Aunt Sheila. "Did Bruce ever know you were going to have a baby?"

"No," said Mom. "I never told anybody but you."

"It's safe with me," said Aunt Sheila, "and of course since Rose hasn't grown up to look like Bruce, nobody's going to guess. Did Tommy ever even wonder?"

"No. He was away on business a lot that year, starting up his company. He never suspected a thing."

"Let's hope you don't run into one of those awful DNA situations, or blood donor things, or genetic illness. What would you do then?"

"Both our families have always been very healthy."

"Except," pointed out Aunt Sheila, "Rose doesn't belong to both your families."

"Well, and that's the thing, Sheila. Tommy must never know."

Speakers roared.

Voices screamed.

Hearts turned over.

"I agree," said Aunt Sheila. "If he knew, it would kill him."

It was the fear that had governed Rose's life for four years: If her father knew, it would kill him.

Which was more terrible? That she was not a Lymond, didn't have Lymond genes, wasn't part of the family she loved? Or that it would kill her father to know?

All the rest of seventh grade, Rose assumed that it would kill Dad to look at her, knowing she was a sham, a stranger; he had not been part of the making of her. When she got older, Rose realized it might be the affair itself that would kill him, and the awful proof of Rose. His wife had once loved a man named Bruce more than she loved her husband, Tommy.

It struck Rose as strange now that she had been angry at Aunt Sheila. In one of her war books — very early war; ancient Greeks or Persians, perhaps — they killed the messenger who brought bad news.

I would have killed Aunt Sheila, she thought, and in my heart, I did. Whereas my mother, who had the affair, I didn't want to kill her.

She knew suddenly that was the reason she liked to read about war. She was at war. It was the reason she liked attacking the root system of an invading marsh grass. She, too, had been invaded.

"Are you listening to me?" shouted Verne.

I'm listening to my genes, thought Rose. They rattle around in me, some stranger's genes. "I'm sorry, Verne. What were you saying?"

We're going to get my brother at the airport, she thought. He's actually my half brother.

She adjusted the treble and bass to normal and then lowered the volume level so they could talk.

Verne watched her hand accomplish that. "I know why you're protecting me," he said, in an odd, proud voice.

That got her attention.

"You had some crush on me, Rose," he said, smiling. His smile did not fade like a normal smile, but continued on, so that Verne was smiling at stop signs and beaming at yellow traffic lights. "I always meant to read your diary, you know, Rose, and see what you said about me. Every time I glanced up from band practice, you were sitting on that top step, hoping I would notice you."

She had never given Verne a thought. It was Alan who absorbed her then and absorbed her now.

"I asked Tabor where you kept the diary," said Verne, "and he even told me where to find the key. But I never got around to it."

His eyes were fixed on the road. A frown was taking

shape above his smiling eyes, splitting him in half. "You saw me working in Frannie Bailey's rock garden," he said. "I was standing between those two weeping spruce trees, with those creepy long-armed branches, and you looked right at me, Rose."

I wish I had a jacket, thought Rose. I'm cold. I'm shivering.

She remembered shivering all the way back to the Y, shivering almost uncontrollably in the locker room, shivering so hard it was difficult to get into her bathing suit. She rejoined the swim class, having missed three quarters of it. The instructor didn't ask for an excuse. Rose didn't offer one.

She remembered the laps. She remembered getting out last, pruny and wrinkled. She had been crying underwater, but nobody knew. She cried in the shower, too, and when she got home her eyes were red and her mother said, "My, there was a lot of chlorine in the pool today, wasn't there?" and her father said, "Rose, I'm going to miss you this weekend. I was looking forward to our movie and popcorn." He told Aunt Sheila, "Rose and I still go to the matinee together. Any minute now she's going to be too old and have better things to do than hang out with her father."

"Go pack, darling," said her mother. "Mr. Lofft will be here in a moment."

And all through that night, alone in the Loffts' strange and murmuring mansion, she had written and written, page after page, trying to get rid of the facts, trying to glue them to the paper, so they wouldn't stick to her.

They stuck.

Verne's jaw was jutting forward, as if he were biting hard on pizza crust and then pulling back to tear it off. It gave him an unpleasant caveman look.

"Frannie Bailey paid real well," said Verne. "And sometimes we'd talk, her and me. But then Milton Lofft showed up and her and Milton Lofft were yelling about money, and yelling about contracts, and when he finally left, she came out of that house saying what she would give for just one smart man. I told her to look no further. I'd take the job. I didn't want to waste time on college. I'm too smart for that. I'm as smart as Bill Gates and those other Harvard dropouts. I could make a billion dollars before I'm thirty, too. I told her about my brains and my plans *and she laughed*, Rose. Frannie Bailey laughed and laughed. She said I needed help to dig manure into topsoil. She said she'd never met anybody who needed college more than I did. She said when she called the landscaping company to get a worker for a few hours, they told her I was on the bottom of their list. They said to wait until she could get somebody else but she said she didn't like waiting."

Verne's words filled the car like cigarette smoke. Rose choked on them. It occurred to Rose that this was a black SUV in which they sat. She squinted at the dashboard. A Dodge Durango. The second witness on I-395 had been corrrect.

For a person who liked to surround herself with facts, she had been rather negligent about acquiring the right ones.

"You've protected me all these years," said Verne, "and don't think I'm not grateful. I heard how you stole a police car so you could hang onto your diary. But they're ganging up on you, Rose. Tabor, your parents, the cops, everybody. They're going to force you to talk, Rose."

His frown had become so intense that his eyes bulged. His face and neck were bright red, like a man playing high notes on a trumpet and running out of air.

Rose tried to ask what he had actually done, and how, but she could not seem to speak. "Frannie Bailey?" she whispered, finally.

"I didn't mean to do it," Verne told her. "I didn't plan it. I just got mad and I acted. That's the kind of guy I am, I don't hang around. I didn't even know it happened until she was lying there."

This could not be true. Frannie Bailey had been killed inside her house, and surely Verne and the rocks and the landscaping project had been outside. Verne had had to follow her in, carrying his rock.

Rose did not want to think about this.

She reached for the door handle but there wasn't one. She ran her fingers over knobs and latches, armrests and protrusions. There was no door handle. It was like the back of the police car. You could get in by yourself. But you couldn't get out by yourself.

"I removed it, Rose," said Verne. "You can't get out."

It was time to take Verne seriously. That had been Frannie Bailey's mistake — not taking Verne seriously. But Rose could think of nothing to say or do. She continued to study the door, unable to believe that it was no longer an exit.

She wondered when he had taken off the door handle. Recently? Just for her? Her mind felt as dislocated as a shoulder. Only the past was becoming clear.

It didn't kill me to know the truth about my parents and it won't kill Dad, either, she thought. It will shock him and sadden him, but we will soldier on, because it will matter to him to be kind. What will kill me is Verne.

So in the end, I suppose my father is never going to know he isn't my father. It took me four years to get to a place where I could think calmly about the truth. But Verne isn't going to give me four years.

The phone in her purse rang.

"Don't answer that," said Verne.

She answered it.

"Rose!" yelled her brother. "What is going on? Alan just reached me. I had to run all the way back to my dorm to look up your cell phone number! Alan has *my* number but nobody has your number. What else is new, Rose? Nobody has your number! I'm a lunatic here! Two thousand miles from whatever you're doing!"

My half brother, thought Rose.

But his was not the voice of somebody half caring. Or half loving. It was the voice of somebody entirely furious and entirely scared.

"Verne killed Frannie Bailey," she told him. "I suppose that's why he dropped out of the band that night.

He really did have other things to do. I think he must be the one who tried to run over me."

She could actually hear her brother swallowing hard. "Where are you now?" he said.

"With Verne in his car."

"God," said her brother prayerfully. "Hand him your phone. Let me talk to him."

"Tabor wants to talk to you, Verne," said Rose, passing the phone, and to her amazement, Verne took it in his right hand and continued to steer haphazardly with his left.

"Tabor, she was protecting me, you know. She always had this huge crush on me. I never knew what to do about it."

It occurred to Rose that Tabor might believe this.

How ghastly. She had been so careful to provide no reason for stealing the police car. What if people really and truly thought the reason for stealing the police car was to protect Verne from a murder charge? What if in some horrid way she was forever bracketed with Verne?

Telling her parents the truth seemed good after all. She even wanted CJ Pierson to know, and Megan Moran, and Craig Gretzak. She wanted Alan and Chrissie and Ming to know.

Up ahead were a lot of emergency lights. They swirled around, heating the pavement, glaring across the intersection, the way they had at her own house only a few weeks ago. It occurred to Rose suddenly that there had been no emergency that day. Questioning her about a four-year-old crime did not require strobe lights.

Those cops were just being hotshots, she thought. Those lights were half the reason I went squirting out of the house like water from a firehose. If they'd been calm, I would have been calm, and none of this would have happened.

She craned her neck to see what was going on ahead of them. Somebody must have had a terrible accident to require so much assistance. Rose twisted in her seat to look behind them and see if an ambulance was coming, in which case she must convince Verne to yield, but behind them were even more police cars.

Verne was still talking to Tabor. Rose had failed to listen in on them. She wondered briefly how she had ever achieved honor roll, she who checked out of listening mode when it mattered.

Verne caught sight of the chaos in front of them. "What is this?" he demanded irritably. He did not slow down, although every car in front of him did. Rose threaded her fingers along the edges of her seat belt, wondering whether the air bag would work, as they were about to crash into several police vehicles. Bad enough I stole one, she thought. Now I'm going to wreck an entire convoy.

At last Verne braked, the car skewing to the left since he was driving one-handed and still talking to Tabor.

"I can see a terrible accident way up the block," said Rose, leaning forward and squinting. "Oh, wow, it looks as if two cars flipped. One is a white van. Verne, it's little kids! They're crying. They're hurt! Oh, Verne, it's really a mess. Those poor people."

The landscaping company had been right to put Verne on the bottom of their list of recommendations. It never occurrred to him that Rose could be lying, that she didn't see one thing farther up the block except more police. She had, however, seen Megan Moran and Craig Gretzak.

Verne came to a full stop.

An officer walked slowly toward them. Verne lowered his window one inch. Through the slit, the officer asked courteously to see Verne's license. Verne told Tabor he'd have to call back and handed Rose the phone.

"Rose," whispered her brother. "Get out of the car."

But Rose could not get out of the car.

"License?" said Verne to the policeman, frowning. "I thought there was an accident."

"Yes, sir. Bad one. Real mess."

Verne twisted in his seat in the way of men who keep their wallets in their back pockets.

He doesn't think he's guilty of anything, thought Rose.

A terrible comparison crept into her thoughts. Her mother, too, never felt guilty of anything. Like Verne, she simply didn't want to be caught.

But I loved her, thought Rose. And I wanted Daddy to go on loving her. I wanted them to love each other. I wanted them both to love me. I was so afraid they would get a divorce and I would be the one and only single and complete reason.

Verne removed a small plastic rectangle from his thin wallet. He handed it through the slit of the window.

"Mind lowering the window a little more, sir?" asked the officer.

It was clear that Verne minded a lot. Rose understood. Opening the window would let the law in, like a breeze.

Verne pressed the button that lowered his window.

The officer's hand was inside immediately, fingers feeling for the lock.

Rose released her shoulder strap.

The click was unmistakable. Verne whipped around. The fingers that had once brought a rock down with sufficient force to break a skull now closed on her wrist with sufficient force to snap it.

But Verne could not prevent his own door from being opened. There was a horrible scrabbling moment of wrestling and grunting.

Frannie Bailey died like that, thought Rose, watching Verne fight. One horrible scrabbling moment and then nothing.

Megan Moran opened Rose's door. She was no weakling, this former basketball player who had made it to Boston. She whacked Verne's knuckles with the handle of her gun and he screamed in pain and let go and Rose was yanked out of the car and onto the pavement and hustled to safety.

Rose thought of happy young men — boys, really — making music in a basement, dreaming of becoming rock stars even though they had only basement talent.

All but one of those boys went on to other talents. This boy . . .

"You lead a very exciting life, Rose," said Megan Moran.

"That has never been my intent," said Rose. She and Megan laughed like old friends.

Perhaps by now they were.

CHAPTER FOURTEEN

"**B**ut how did you know to set up a roadblock for Verne?" asked Rose.

"Alan called us," said Megan. "Almost too late, but that seems to be your lifestyle."

"*Alan called you?*" She was astonished. How could Alan possibly have known who and what the danger was?

"Yup. Letter A in the book of crushes."

"It was not a book of crushes," said Rose stiffly. "It was a diary."

Megan Moran looked skeptical. She changed the subject. "May I ask why you got into a car of the type that tried to run you over? In fact, the *actual* car that tried to run you over? Anjelica says you couldn't even remember the driver's name. Yet you cut school and drove off with him."

"Well, I sort of knew him," said Rose. "Anyway, it worked out in the end."

"Risky," said Megan Moran.

"Basketball players should be comfortable with risk," said Rose.

"Basketball is a game. Murder is not."

Rose had no response to this. Poor choices seemed to be her specialty.

Megan Moran suddenly put an arm around Rose and hugged her, as if they were sisters, or team-mates.

The intersection was now immobilized by police. Traffic was being intercepted and directed down other blocks. The police were listening to long, earnest explanations from Verne, whose hands were fastened behind his back. His metal cuffs gleamed in the sunlight. Every car motioned by took its time, hoping to figure out what was going on. SUVs had the distinct advantage of being high enough for a good view. Rose didn't care how high up off the road they were; strangers were never going to figure this one out.

To her surprise, two vehicles were suddenly waved through. The first was Alan's, big and square and dark. Chrissie was waving madly out the passenger window. The second vehicle, a small, pale shadow of the first, was Anjelica Lofft's.

Anjelica parked where the police told her to, but Alan steered around the police and pulled up, as had a number of vehicles before him in the last few days, at Rose's side. Chrissie had to run around the whole car to reach Rose, but Alan had only to step out, so he got there first, hugging Rose fiercely, but not as if he liked her. It was the hug of somebody who wanted to be sure she was still alive and breathing before he crushed her ribs. The hug of a big brother's friend.

"You're crazy," said Alan, just as Tabor would have wanted him to. "I would have had a heck of a time explaining to Tabor why I let you get killed."

"She isn't crazy," said Chrissie, just as Rose would have wanted Chrissie to. "She really didn't see anything and she really didn't know anything. So there." The girls finished hugging and Chrissie said, "But really, Rose, Alan is absolutely right. Getting into a black SUV after a black SUV tried to kill you! You *are* crazy."

Anjelica was joining them, so Rose could not explain that going with Verne had been a handy escape from having to talk to Anjelica. "I didn't even glance at what Verne drove," she admitted. "It seemed logical that Tabor would fly home early. And he'd call a buddy to pick him up because Mom and Dad were at work. And he'd want me to meet him, since I was his reason for coming home."

Verne was being placed in the backseat of a police car. An officer's hand pressed down on top of Verne's head, forcing him to bend, just like on TV. And even though they were only a hundred feet away, and even though they knew what was happening, and to whom, and why, it remained just as unreal as TV.

"I'm having trouble imagining Verne as a murderer," said Alan. "I was fourteen and he was eighteen when Tabor had the band. Anybody who was a high school senior, I pretty much respected."

"It wasn't Tabor's band, though," said Chrissie

slowly. "It was Verne's. It must have crushed Verne when it turned into Tabor's. Proof that Verne couldn't even run a basement band."

"Why did Verne kill Frannie Bailey?" asked Anjelica.

Rose shook her head. "For no reason. Verne told her that he was smart enough to be her business partner instead. She laughed and said he was way too dumb. His feelings were hurt. So he killed her."

Anjelica had tears in her eyes. "I loved Frannie," she said. "She could be very blunt. She hurt everybody's feelings. Routinely. But to kill her! Oh, Rose, you are so lucky to have escaped."

When Verne's fighting feet and hands had been corralled in the back of the squad car, the police shut the door and he was trapped. Rose knew how it felt. Knew the smell and the sense of horror. "I don't think Verne would really have done anything to me," she said. "He was calm. He thought —" But Rose didn't want them to know that Verne thought she loved him. And she didn't want to talk about the passenger door he had fixed so that she could never leave.

Anjelica sniffed. "Verne was probably calm when he cracked Frannie over the head. He was probably calm driving on 395, examining the trash crew to see who was the girl with blond hair. He's probably calm during all his homicidal moments."

Alan was laughing. "You know, Anjelica, you're okay."

Exactly what I need, thought Rose. Alan falling in love with Anjelica.

• • •

Chrissie Klein imagined that Friday night drive in the brown Navigator.

Mr. Lofft, steaming from his fight with Frannie Bailey. Finding himself in Friday evening traffic: hostile and edgy and even lawless. Screaming at the windshield, seeing nothing.

Anjelica, saddled with a silent houseguest, not distracted by videos or blue corn chips.

Rose, staring mutely out the side window, seeing nothing. What Rose could not see was her future. How to go on in a family that was only half hers?

But what Milton Lofft could not see was a human being standing at the side of the road. He saw only his goal: a turnpike entrance. Why should a man of Milton Lofft's stature have to wait another sixty seconds? How could Milton Lofft endure the blockade of ordinary traffic as if he were an ordinary person? Naturally, he pulled far to the right, drove over the curb, and accelerated across the grass.

And what had Anjelica seen?

Not enough to be one hundred percent sure, or she wouldn't have tried to tap into Rose's memory. But enough to worry that her beloved father had killed a pedestrian and gone on without stopping.

There were two parts to such a crime: the driving part, and the driving away part. The second was so much worse. To leave a bleeding body. Give no aid. Make no calls. Milton Lofft had driven home so fast and furiously because he believed — and he was right — that he could put it behind him.

At the lake estate, he let the girls out at the front door and drove on alone to his garage. Evidence would be on his bumper or fender or broken headlight, but Mr. Lofft need never touch the car again or let anybody else touch it, because indeed he was not an ordinary man with the ordinary number of vehicles. He could give his mechanics a nice bonus and let them go; take up horses and gardens instead. After enough time passed, he could have the car crushed into a block of metal.

The worst that could happen to Rose was a collective shudder from the Lymonds. Probably a lot of shudders from her father. But Rose was nearly sixteen, a long time to be a daughter, granddaughter, great-granddaughter. They loved her. She was theirs. They'd get past this sad little story and forget about it.

Anjelica could not forget.

Only Chrissie Klein, Alan Finney, and Anjelica Lofft knew what Rose had half said in her diary. But that diary no longer existed and the author of the diary did not seem to recall the bump in the road.

From television court shows, Chrissie knew that any statement of hers would not be admissible. She'd be quoting her thirteen-year-old self quoting the scribbles of a twelve-year-old. Which didn't exist. There was no proof, there could never be proof. In an American court, a really good guess wasn't good enough.

Alan's eyes were fixed on Rose, no longer some-body's little sister annoying the big kids but a woman of mystery and action. Chrissie had a feeling she didn't have to worry about Rose or Alan.

But Anjelica . . .

Justice required that Milton Lofft be investigated. But mercy required that Anjelica be spared a larger burden.

Among her confirmation class requirements had been memorizing a verse from the Book of Micah. *And what doth the Lord require of thee, but to do justly and love mercy?*

That's Rose, thought Chrissie. Trying to do justly and love mercy.

So Chrissie said, "What a relief for you, Anjelica. Now you don't have to worry that your father killed Frannie Bailey."

Anjelica Lofft glared at Chrissie Klein. "I never worried that my father killed Frannie Bailey," she said icily. "I was present, as you recall, and I knew perfectly well he didn't kill Frannie Bailey."

"But I didn't know anything," said Rose. "How come all of you knew something and I didn't? Chrissie, I can't understand why you and Alan were even thinking of me. And I don't know what you wanted, Anjelica, since you never did worry that your father was involved."

Chrissie tried to look like a Barbie doll, smooth and wide-eyed.

Alan turned red.

Anjelica stared toward the distance as if modeling for a photo shoot.

Megan Moran folded her arms.

Chrissie broke first. "Oh, Rose," she blurted, "I read your diary way back at that slumber party. You kept saying you didn't see anything and I didn't believe you, and I sneaked in and read it. So when you took the police car, I knew why. I thought you did the right thing. And even though the police told me you might be in danger, I knew you couldn't be, because your secret didn't have anything to do with Frannie Bailey's murder."

Back in the car with Verne, Rose had been ready to tell everybody her secret. She wasn't ready anymore. She felt as if Chrissie had nailed her to some wall.

"You know I read it," said Anjelica. "For your sake I've hated Aunt Sheila all this time. In seventh grade the next week, I couldn't face you, because I knew things that I had no right to know."

Rose found it surprisingly bracing that Anjelica had loathed Aunt Sheila for her sake. "But why," asked Rose, "did you keep my secret when the police came to talk to your father? You could have cleared up the whole thing."

There was a funny little pause, in which Chrissie and Alan seemed to participate.

Anjelica said, "You and I weren't friends, Rose. I didn't know how to be a friend back in seventh grade But staying silent seemed like what a friend would do."

Staying silent, thought Rose. No longer a choice with my parents.

She looked at Alan.

"Okay," said Alan, shifting his weight from foot to foot, licking his lips, and tugging at the neckline of his sweatshirt. He looked approximately one hundred times more guilty of something than Verne had looked. "Okay, so, Rose, so don't hate my guts."

"I could never hate your guts," she said. Or anything else about you, she thought, the old crush flaring up like a bonfire.

"Yeah, well, that's about to change," said Alan. "See, I read the diary, too. The last dozen pages anyway."

Alan had read her book of crushes? Rose's blush covered her entire body.

"I mean, in the kitchen, you acted as if I'd belted you in the jaw when all I did was mention the word 'diary.' I figured you had some serious secret in that thing and I thought it would be all blood and gore and crushed skulls. I didn't know the fatality would be your own family."

I won't cry, thought Rose.

"So here's the thing," said Alan, without taking a breath or pausing between words, "this is why you're going to hate me, Rose, it's because I told Megan Moran what was in the diary, see, because when I called the police, I was afraid they'd think you were protecting Verne and they wouldn't worry enough, and what if they didn't act fast? Because I was positive Verne meant to run you over and he'd convince you to lie down under his car and change the oil or something and I could picture you thinking of Civil War battles instead of noticing that you were getting squashed, so I called my sister Cecily, who was at St. Mary's with Megan Moran, and Cecily said, 'Trust Megan,' so I did."

So the police knew. Rose Lymond was right back where she had started. She might as well have let the police keep the diary.

Another car arrived. The familiar Crown Vic, driven by CJ Pierson. Her father was in front, hand on the dash, looking everywhere for Rose.

"Your mother's office is on the far side of the city, so it'll be another half hour before she gets here," said Megan Moran, "but Detective Pierson picked up your dad."

"You told Dad about my diary?"

"No. That's your choice. But you know what, Rose? All your father will care about is that you're safe."

The Crown Vic was pulling up close. The door was flung open, and her father jumped out before it stopped and ran to Rose and enveloped her. His arms were tighter than they had been since she was about five, when hugs really could keep away the scary things. He kept thanking everybody, hugging her again, saying incredulously, "*Verne?*" and hugging her more.

Megan Moran rounded up Alan and Chrissie and Anjelica like stray kindergartners and nudged them toward their cars.

CJ Pierson suggested that Rose and her father sit in the Crown Vic for a while. He had to check on a detail or two with the other police. Then he'd drive them home.

Rose and her father got in. When they shut the door, it was like shutting out the world.

Rose thought her father could have slumped there for days without talking, just keeping his arm around her and knowing that she was warm and safe. But Megan Moran had been generous enough to let Rose know she had only half an hour before Mom arrived. It was a big topic to cover in half an hour. "Daddy, I'm going to tell you what I wrote in the diary."

"Okay." He didn't even look worried. He probably figured that since his baby girl hadn't been murdered after all, there were no worries left in the parent list.

"And when I'm done," Rose told him, "you're not going to love me the way you did."

"That would be impossible."

"Maybe." Rose found herself imitating Alan, breathing deeply, fiddling with her collar.

"That bad, huh?" Her father was smiling.

"Yes," she said briefly. "So that November. Friday. Four years ago. I skipped swim class. I came home early. Aunt Sheila and Mom were in the kitchen, talking about things I hadn't known. I blamed Aunt Sheila, but the blame belongs to Mom. If blame matters. And what I wrote in the diary, and what I had to destroy so nobody else could read it, was what they said. I'm sorry,

Daddy. I don't want to be the one who tells you. I'm sorry anybody has to tell you."

Now he was alarmed.

"I'm not your daughter. I'm not a Lymond. Mom had an affair the year you were starting up your business. I'm a stranger's child. Not yours."

"Oh, that," said her father.

CHAPTER FIFTEEN

"**O**h, *that?*" repeated Rose. She was almost furious. How could he dismiss this? This was supposed to have killed him. This had been her nightmare for four years.

She pulled out of his hug and twisted to stare into his eyes.

"I know about the affair, sweetheart. I've always known. It means nothing. You've been my daughter from the day we brought you home from the hospital. I wouldn't change a hair on your head. In fact, I'm grateful to your biological father. Otherwise, you wouldn't be you."

"But, Daddy, I'm not a Lymond."

"Yes, you are. Sometimes you're so much like your great-grandmother I start laughing." He pulled her hair into a ponytail and brushed her face with it, as if she were six years old and worried about her teddy bear. "If I had guessed that that was the secret in your diary . . . but I never would have, because you're so completely mine I forget the facts. Rose, this was my fault. I never sat you down to talk. You had to find out in a shabby way, lurking in a back door. You thought you were somebody else's all this time, honey? Well, you're not. You're mine."

He pulled out his white cotton handkerchief, stiff with the creases Mom had ironed into it, and dried Rose's tears. "Right now it's also my fault you almost got killed by Verne. I can't believe he tried to run you over. How many pizzas did I supply that kid with? How many times did I give him gas money?"

How could Dad change the subject? How could he possibly care about Verne under these circumstances? "Verne thought I had a crush on him," she said crossly. "He thought I was protecting him. Yuck. Well, who cares about him? Daddy, I'm afraid of what Nannie and everybody else will think about — well — what Aunt Sheila said. Because even the police know now. It turns out Alan and Chrissie read my diary. I don't care about them, though, they're okay. But what about Mopsy and Popsy and Aunt Laura and Nannie and all the rest of our family?"

"I never talked about it, Rose, and they never asked. New Englanders, you know. We like to let things lie there, hidden under the autumn leaves, so to speak. But I'm pretty sure my parents and my sister and my grandmother all know. They wouldn't have told your cousins and certainly I've never spoken to your brother. If Alan knew all this time and Tabor didn't, maybe I'd better bring Tabor home early for real. He'll love that."

"But Aunt Sheila —"

"— is an idiot."

Rose began to laugh and then to cry. "Mom said it would kill you to find out. That's why I kept the secret, Daddy. I thought it would kill you."

He held her tightly and then he had to let go, because they both knew now that no parent could build a complete fence around his child — and no child could build a complete fence around her parent.

"It could have killed me, I suppose. Tabor was a toddler, work was so demanding, life seemed so good — and my wife found somebody else. But it didn't crush me. It brought me you."

"Weren't you furious with Mom?"

"Sure. But I let go of it."

I didn't let myself be furious, either, she thought. I've inherited traits from Dad even without genes. "What about *him*?" she said.

"Since I love you, Rose," he said, "how furious can I be about *him*?"

"We haven't used his name."

"Let's not. For years I had this nightmare that he'd return and claim you and somehow, in the viciousness of courts and lawyers, I'd lose my precious daughter to some stranger. But you're too old for that now. I can stop worrying."

It had never crossed Rose's mind that her father was the one worrying. She leaned on him. After a while, she realized that he was leaning on her, too.

"Tell me if you want to meet him, honey."

"Eeeeeeeeeuuuh!" shrieked Rose. "No!"

They laughed. "Another nightmare set to rest," said her father.

Any minute Mom would arrive. There was still so much to say. "You and Mom never talked about it?" she asked.

"Not once. She doesn't know that I know." He swished her ponytail again. "I guess you inherit your skill at silence from me."

We *are* alike. I *am* his. Instead of sorrow, Rose began to feel joy. "Why didn't Mom guess that I myself was the secret I stayed silent for?"

"I suspect your mother has more or less forgotten. She's quick to forgive herself, you know," he said wryly. "When I think of you coming to terms with that all by yourself! Oh, Rose! I'm so sorry."

"You know what, Dad?" And the truth of what she was about to say astonished even Rose. "It wasn't that big of a deal. Life swept on. In fact, I forgot, too. I guess I'm just as much Mom's daughter as I am yours. Then when the police had the diary and I remembered what I'd written, I fell apart. I couldn't let anybody read it. I had to take action." They were laughing helplessly. "Pretty dumb action," she admitted.

"I'm almost proud of you now, stealing that police car."

"I still have forty-four hours of community service left."

"My daughter, the delinquent," he said. "We'll need Mom's advice on the next step. Whether we go back to the judge or what. Are you pretty angry with your mother, Rose? You don't act like it."

"You know what, Daddy? I never really got mad. I managed to be mad at Aunt Sheila instead."

"I never liked Sheila anyway," said her father. "I was grateful she stuck to her own coast. Rose, when your mother gets here, she'll take her cues from you. She always does. If you're cool about it, she'll forgive herself by dinnertime."

"I wonder what we're having," said Rose. "I skipped breakfast because it's been that kind of week and I skipped lunch because of driving away with Verne. I'm starving, Dad. I'm still thinking about the French toast I didn't have on Sunday."

Her father laughed. "I guess we're going to be okay," he said. "Because when the biggest problem is what to have for dinner, life is pretty good."

Life *is* pretty good, thought Rose Lymond. I'm alive. I'm a goddess at school. Tabor likes me enough to go berserk on the phone when I'm riding around with a killer. Alan likes me enough to run after me when I'm in danger. Chrissie's still my true friend. Anjelica — well, who knows what that was about?

The important thing is, my father is my father.

He always was.

He always will be.

ABOUT THE AUTHOR

Caroline B. Cooney lives in a small seacoast village in Connecticut. She writes every day and then takes a long walk on the beach to figure out what she's going to write the following day. She's written more than seventy books for young people, including *The Party's Over*; the acclaimed The Face on the Milk Carton quartet; *Flight #116 Is Down*, which won the 1994 Golden Sower Award for Young Adults, the 1995 Rebecca Caudill Young Readers' Book Award, and was selected as an ALA Recommended Book for the Reluctant Young Adult Reader; *Flash Fire*; *Emergency Room*; *The Stranger*; and *Twins*. *Wanted!* and *The Terrorist* were both 1998 ALA Quick Picks for Reluctant Young Adult Readers.

Ms. Cooney reads as much as possible and has three grown children and two granddaughters.